# *Lyranel's Song*

## *Leslie Carmichael*

Blooming Tree Press
Austin, Texas

Lyranel's Song

Blooming Tree Press
P.O. Box 140934
Austin, Texas 78714-0934

Cover art by Elsbet Vance
Cover and Book design by Kelly Bell
Logo by Tabi Designs
Editor - Madeline Smoot
Copy editing by Peggy Brandt
Library of Congress Catalog Card Number: 2005922454
ISBN: 0-9718348-5-7 (hardcover)
ISBN: 0-9718348-6-5 (softcover)
www.bloomingtreepress.com



Blooming Tree Press
P.O. Box 140934
Austin, Texas, 78714-0934

Printed in the United States of America.

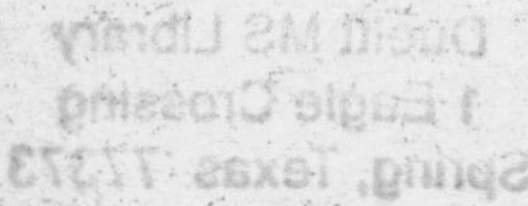

# *Dedication*

*For my family:*

*Duncan, Ariane, Jade and Wayne*


# *Acknowledgements:*

With many thanks to the current and former members of the KooKoos critique group: Gloria Singendonk, Alma Fullerton, Lori Robidoux, Laurie Brown, Lisa Marta, Linda Joy Singleton and Trina Wiebe. Also thanks to instructor Cathy Beveridge, the Imaginative Fiction Writers' Association; and the members of the Symon's Valley United Church choir, for teaching me the joy of song.

I would also like to thank my editor, Madeline Smoot, for all of her great suggestions, Elsbet Vance for her lovely illustrations; and Miriam Hees, for believing in me.

N
W
E
S
Yasur Sea
Mayette
Delta
Candelo
Castle Trioste
Blue River
White River
Giles River
Castle Candelo
Trioste
Sir Thomas' Manor
The Ruins
The Fens
Gold River
Gavanton
Gnoti Lake
Marfol
Western Ocean
Siella
Vierre
The Great River
Castle Siella
Castle Vierre
Cansu River
Middle Sea

# *Book One*

# *Gift*

# Chapter One

It was dark when Lyranel woke. She hooked a finger over the edge of her bed curtain and peeked out. Shadowy lumps filled her room, slowly growing into familiar shapes of chair and dressing table in the purple-gray predawn light from her window. She thought she had heard someone calling her, but there was no one there.

Lyranel pulled the heavy velvet curtain aside, letting in a gust of cold air. She shivered as she struggled into her fur-lined robe and then reached for her crutches. Shoving her lumpy feet into thick felt slippers, she rose, then hobbled across the room.

She frowned. Was something moving outside? Her bay window, on the castle's second floor, looked out over the enclosed courtyard, with its dormant apple trees and snow-covered gardens. She knew the servants were usually up before dawn, but surely no one would be out in the bitter cold. Perhaps it was only the darkness playing tricks on her.

Lyranel unlatched the left-hand pane and opened it. Icy air swirled in as she peered into the courtyard. There was nothing there. She lifted her gaze and stared toward the east, where the sun was just now rising, turning the world pink with promise.

She gasped. A surge of… something… rippled through her.

As the sun lifted its pale head above the horizon, the Song burst out of her. It had no words, but she knew that it was a Song of welcome for the morning, a quiet, joyful melody that grew from deep inside. The world brightened as she Sang. A small clump of fir trees in one corner of the courtyard seemed to take on a greener hue, and the snow sparkled like diamonds. A few stray green buds even popped out on some of the apple trees.

Lyranel slapped one hand over her mouth, cutting off the sound. She swayed, then half-fell into the cushioned seat below the window. She had cut the Song off as soon as she realized what she was doing, but it was too late.

She knew what it meant. She was a Singer.

"Oh, warts," she said.

She gulped in a breath. Had anyone heard her? Usually, any noise from her room roused her nursemaid, Nan, as if it were a rooster's crow. She listened for footsteps in the hall, but heard only silence.

"Lyranel?" The voice came from outside. Lyranel slowly rose from the cushion and looked down at the courtyard. Paul, the fourteen-year-old kitchen boy, stood there staring up at her. "Was that you?"

"Don't tell anyone!" said Lyranel.

Paul's Adam's apple bobbed up and down as he swallowed. "No, of course not."

"Is anyone with you?" she asked.

"No, no one," he replied. "I'm the only one out here."

"Good," Lyranel breathed. "We have to keep it secret!"

"Don't worry, I won't tell," said Paul. "You know I won't."

She nodded. They had kept each other's secrets ever since she had befriended him when he first came to the castle. "I know."

"Well," he grinned. "Happy birthday, anyway."

"Birthday?" Her mouth dropped open in astonishment. It was her twelfth birthday today, Saint Stephen's Day, the day after Christmas. How could she have forgotten? Paul's grin widened as he watched her.

"Oh, you," she said. He waved, started to walk away, then stopped and looked up at her again.

"Lyranel?" he said. "It was... wonderful."

"Hmph!" she said as she slammed the window shut.



There was a rap on Lyranel's door, and she gasped. Before she could answer, Nan's bulky figure backed into her room, dark brown skirts swaying. She turned around and beamed at Lyranel, her arms full of fabric.

"Good morning, my chick," said Nan. "My, but you're awake early today. Not surprising, I suppose. Couldn't sleep for excitement, eh?"

Lyranel swallowed, then nodded.

"I was up early too, talking to Cook," Nan continued, laying the bundle of linens she was carrying on the bench beside Lyranel. "I must say, I haven't felt this spry in years.

And what a lovely day for your feast. Well, off with you now, get dressed! You've a long day ahead of you."

That was true enough. At twelve, she was finally old enough to take up her duties as Lady of the Castle, a title that she would keep until she became Duchess. Lyranel's father, Duke Trioste, would this evening be formally presenting her to the assembled folk: nobles, servants and townsmen alike. She would take the oath and be given the keys to the stillroom, stores and pantry, which Nan had held ever since Lyranel's mother had died.



Carrying the keys meant that Lyranel would be in charge of much of the organization of the castle, keeping an eye on supplies, medicines and foods. Alistair, the Duke's seneschal and master of ceremonies, had been training her since she was eight. Of course, she wouldn't be doing it alone, not for several more years.

Her father had been reluctant to let her take the rank. He hadn't even wanted her to be one of his pages when she was six, but she had pestered him night and day, insisting that it was the only way for her to learn. She had felt so proud in the black and red page's uniform when she had succeeded in convincing him. And after that, he had treated her just like the other pages, his only concession to her disability being to let her sit down more often than the rest of them.

"Well?" Nan demanded, startling her. "Get a move on, pet."

Lyranel reached for her crutches and rose from the cushioned window seat. Her feet didn't hurt as much today as they usually did. She went to her wooden wardrobe and picked out an overdress. Balancing against the door, she slipped the high-necked green gown over her head and pulled it down. A wriggle of her hips settled the dress into place. Its hem was long enough to cover her feet. She shoved them back into her fat felt slippers and wished, as she did every day, that she could wear dainty ladies' shoes instead.



Lyranel had been born with clubbed feet, both of them turned inwards. The town's herbwomen had all said she would grow out of it. But when Lyranel still hadn't at six months of age, her father had listened to the fateful suggestion of a wandering chirurgeon whom he had welcomed into the castle. The man had been respectable-looking and seemed to know his medicine. He had broken the bones of

Lyranel's feet and ankles, insisting that was the only way she could hope to walk normally. Nan had told Lyranel that she had screamed for weeks with pain. In anger, the Duke had exiled the chirurgeon off his lands.

Lyranel's feet had healed oddly. The knowledge that gentle manipulation would have worked better had come far too late for her. It was also too late for her mother's Singing to help, even if she could have. Unfortunately, Lady Miriana's Songs had not had any effect, though she had tried her best.



Nan padded up behind her. "Just let me do your hair, dear," she said.

Lyranel nodded and made her way to the dressing table with its antique mirror. The table, like much of her furniture, had belonged to Miriana. Nan undid Lyranel's long russet hair from its braid and began brushing it with strong, even strokes as Lyranel watched in the mirror. The glass made her face look a little spotty.

Nan sighed. "Oh, you're getting to be so much like her."

"Who?" asked Lyranel.

"Why, your mother of course, chick," said Nan. "You have her lovely brown eyes. And her hair." She smiled at Lyranel in the mirror. "You have much in common with her."

Including being a Singer, thought Lyranel. Lady Miriana had been an exceptional Singer, she'd heard. Well, overheard, really. No one would talk to her about it directly, for fear of the Duke finding out. But she'd eavesdropped on enough conversations to gather that her mother had been a fine and powerful Singer before her death, and that was why the duchy had prospered so.



Singers didn't sing ordinary songs. There was magic in their music. No birth, death, marriage, or other celebration was complete without Singing, for the magic of the Songs evoked the spirits that resided in everything: the people, the animals, the plants and rocks—even the very air itself—and kept them in harmony. Singers were welcome everywhere.

Not here in Trioste, however. Music wasn't forbidden, but no one was allowed to Sing. The simple tunes of the peasants were all right, and the Duke did allow hymns in chapel and church. Lyranel loved listening to both, especially the hymns. Sometimes Lyranel thought the sacred music was very close to being magical itself. Yesterday's carols during the Christ Mass service had been more enchanting than usual. The notes had wrapped around her like a soft blanket, warming her heart. Even her father had looked more peaceful than he had in weeks.

The land of Trioste hadn't been very well balanced since Lady Miriana's and her guard's death in a rockfall when Lyranel had been two years old. The Duke had banned all Singers after that and the banishment still held. Trioste prospered, but not nearly as well as before. Crops died for no good reason. Animals of the forest became scarce, and herds of sheep got more than their fair share of illnesses.

Lyranel had never been brave enough to ask why her father hated Singers so much. Every time she had mentioned the subject, people suddenly found other things to do, or had urgent appointments.

"We'll just do this for now," said Nan, re-braiding Lyranel's hair, and tying it off with a bit of leather cord. "I'll make it a bit fancier later on, when it's time for the ceremony.

You'll need to look perfect then so that you don't disgrace your father."

Lyranel winced. If her father knew she was a Singer, it wouldn't matter how she looked.

# Chapter Two

Lyranel's father, Duke Trioste, was already in the dining room when she arrived. He liked to start the day with a hearty breakfast, for he often rode about inspecting land and livestock, ruling over disputes and overseeing the businesses that made Trioste wealthy. He usually didn't have time for more than a bit of bread and meat for his mid-day meal, eaten in the saddle and washed down with ale.



This morning he was dressed in his "working outfit" of wool trousers and linen tunic, in his customary black. His only jewelry was a gold ducal signet ring. A thin gold band circled his head to signify his rank, instead of the heavy coronet of gold strawberry leaves. His black hair was tied back in a short braid.

Lyranel dropped into her seat and allowed Janissara, one of the newer pages, to hang her crutches from the hook set into the wall just behind her.

Duke Trioste dribbled hot wax from a candle into a puddle at the bottom of the document that he was reading.

He pulled off his ring and set the raised design into the wax, sealing it with the family crest of a bear standing on its hind legs, then tossed the paper onto a growing pile and picked up another.

"Good morning, Lyranel," he said.

"G-good morning, father," said Lyranel. She wondered if he was going to ask his usual question about her plans for the day, but he was silent.

Janissara was hovering behind Lyranel with a plate of eggs and baked ham. Her small hand trembled as she slid the heavy plate onto the table. Janissara poured water into Lyranel's goblet, spilling only a little, then retreated to the sideboard to stand at lip-biting attention. The eggs were fluffy and scrambled with a bit of white cheese, and the cubes of ham smelled of cinnamon. Lyranel smiled, remembering how nervous she had been when she was a page as she reached for a piece of warm spiced bread from the basket in front of her. It was only then that she noticed the neatly-wrapped package above her place setting.

She glanced at her father, but he seemed intent on the document of thin, yellow vellum.

Lyranel carefully removed the rich cloth from the parcel. It was a diadem! Lacy strawberry leaves of polished silver wire fanned out across the triangular front, which rose to a graceful point in the middle. The tiara was a lighter, more delicate version of her father's heavy ducal coronet, and obviously intended for a Lady.

Duke Trioste cleared his throat. "Well?" He had lowered the vellum.

"It's beautiful," said Lyranel.

"I thought you might wear it this evening, when I grant you your new status. It is appropriate."



"Oh, yes! Thank you, father."

"You're welcome." He went back to reading the document. "And… happy birthday."

Lyranel turned the diadem over, admiring it. Facets cut into the wire made it sparkle in the light from the dining room's high windows. She wondered if it might have been her mother's, but it looked too new. Sure enough, there was the maker's mark stamped on the inside rim, from a silversmith in the town below the castle, who had only set up shop there about five years ago.

As Lady of the Castle, Lyranel would be entitled to wear the diadem during official functions. She pictured it perched proudly on her head at feasts and when welcoming honored guests to the castle.

Except that she might not be doing that now. If her father found out that she was a Singer, he would have to banish her. He would probably be glad to be rid of her. And where could she go, alone and on crutches? Perhaps he would let her take her pony, Jewel. With a sigh, she placed the pretty thing back on the table.



"God's wounds!" Duke Trioste spat.

Lyranel jerked, startled. "Father?"

"A letter. With bad news."

"Oh." Lyranel contemplated her meal. If she were banished, what would she find to eat, all on her own? She would certainly miss Cook's good meals.

"Lyranel? Are you not interested?" her father asked. Lyranel looked at him. He was watching her, his brows drawn down in a frown. "You usually pester me for details."

"I'm sorry, father. I was… thinking about something else."

"Lyranel, if you're to be Lady of the Castle," said Duke Trioste, "you should always know what is happening. In case there is something you must prepare us for."

Lyranel looked down at her plate. "Yes, father."

"Hm. This is from Duke Vierre. Do you know who he is?"

"Of course," said Lyranel. "He is the Duke of the duchy to the south and east of ours and a member of the Compact of Four. Our lands do not touch, except at one corner."



"And the Compact is?"

Lyranel took a breath. He had a habit of testing her, to see how much she knew.

"Centuries ago, there were people called the Invader Kings. The Dukes and Duchesses of Siella, Trioste, Candelo and Vierre destroyed the Kings and vowed that there would never be another kingdom here. They also decided that those who reigned would always take the name of their duchy, when they took office. Like you. I will too, when I become Duchess of Trioste."

"Very good. Anything else?"

"Um. Duke Vierre's daughter is named Sapphira, who will succeed him and take the name after her father dies. She has a younger brother named Mikal."

"I see Alistair has taught you well. I shall have to update him, however. The boy may end up inheriting," said Lyranel's father.

"Why?"

"Vierre also reports that his daughter has been acting oddly."

"But why would that mean she couldn't inherit?"



Her father flicked his gaze over the top of the paper at her. "There is… a history of madness in their family. Duke Vierre's father ended his days hearing voices inside his head and insisting that he was made of glass. He never went out, for fear of breaking. Vierre doesn't say outright that this is what is happening to his daughter, but I can read between the lines. He's worried, I can tell."

Lyranel opened her mouth, then closed it again. Sapphira, she knew, was also a powerful Singer. They weren't banned in Duke Vierre's lands, but she didn't want to mention it to her father. Instead, she said, "Thank you for telling me."

"You're welcome. I judge it useful knowledge for a Lady of the Castle."

Lyranel gave him a lopsided smile.

"So. This letter states that the Duke is becoming concerned about what seems to be a plague encroaching on the northern edge of his lands," said her father. "Some sort of blight is killing his farmers' fields. Animals and humans in the area are sickening and dying as well."



"That's terrible!" said Lyranel. "What's causing it?"

Duke Trioste shook his head. "He doesn't know. But it seems to be affecting Candelo to our east, as well. Vierre thinks that it might even be coming from there. Though it is odd that we haven't received anything from Duke Candelo concerning it. Vierre has not been able to find out more, as men who are sent into the stricken areas... do not come out alive. He asks if we are experiencing the same problem."

"Are we?" asked Lyranel.

"No," he said. "At least not that I know of. I suppose I shall have to send someone to our eastern border to check. But they will have to be careful. Vierre states that the sickness comes upon people quickly, usually without any warning. Sometimes there is no way to tell that an area is diseased until they are in it."

"Is there a way to protect them?"

"Vierre says not." Her father's eyes narrowed. "Can you think of any suggestions?"



Lyranel gazed around the sunlit room, looking for inspiration. Disease seemed impossible, in such calm surroundings. She flicked a glance at her father, who was waiting for her answer. It was another test, she knew. She could think of nothing.

"I'm sorry, father. I don't know."

He raised one of his eyebrows at her. "The animals which have sickened are the ones that humans have forced to remain penned in the area, like cows and chickens," he said. "Other animals seem to know, and they try to avoid the place where it will happen. Dogs seem particularly sensitive to it."

"Well… if you sent some dogs with each patrol, perhaps they could help the humans stay away from the sick patches," said Lyranel. "The dogs could warn them."

Her father smiled. "Precisely. Very good, Lyranel. I shall so order it."

With a nod, he gathered up the rest of the documents and rose, then left the room with them bundled under his arm.

Lyranel let out a breath. "Warts," she muttered.

"Milady?" asked Janissara.



Lyranel shook her head. "Nothing, Janissara."

Lyranel spooned up a bite and chewed slowly. She had gotten through this meal without revealing her new talent, at least. Old Cate, the storyteller, had once told Lyranel that being a Singer was considered a gift, but to Lyranel it seemed more of a curse.

Old Cate had also said that Singers sometimes couldn't control themselves. They Sang whether they wanted to or not. Well, Lyranel would just have to make sure that didn't happen. She resolved to clamp down on any urge in that direction.

Lyranel finished her breakfast in quick bites, washing them down with water. She wiped her face with her linen napkin and beckoned to Janissara.

"More water, milady?" the girl asked.

"No, thank you, Janissara," said Lyranel. "I would like to take a basket of food up to Old Cate's cave today. It is St. Stephen's day, after all. There will be plenty left over from yesterday's Christmas feast."

"Can she not come to the gatehouse like everyone else to receive her gifts of charity?" asked Janissara.



"She is old, Janissara, and cannot walk the path so easily in winter," said Lyranel.

Janissara eyed the crutches behind Lyranel, probably thinking that the path up the mountain behind the castle would not be so easy for Lyranel either.

"It's very slippery out there," she said.

Janissara, who was only eight years old and the daughter of one of the Duke's border nobles, was new to the castle. She hadn't yet learned that Lyranel didn't let her disability slow her down. Certainly, there were some things Lyranel couldn't do – some games were impossible, and long stairwells were difficult – but she could do most everything else.

"I will be fine. Nan accompanies me and Paul will carry the basket." She reached for her crutches and stood. "And I am quite agile by now. I've been on these crutches all my life, you know. Tell Cook to make sure the basket is a good big one, please."

"Yes, milady," said Janissara.

Lyranel headed for the door, swinging her legs between the crutches so quickly that Janissara's mouth dropped open in surprise.

# Chapter Three

"There's something different about you today," said Old Cate.

Lyranel stared at her. Old Cate couldn't possibly know about the Singing. Could she? Lyranel hadn't mentioned anything about it!

She forced a laugh. "Well, yes. I'm Lady of the Castle now. Or I will be this evening."

"Well," said Old Cate, "I suppose you are right. Still..."

Nan, who had settled onto the hard bench next to the wall, suddenly let out a loud snore. Her hands were folded over her ample belly, and she was solidly asleep.

"Dear old Nan," said Old Cate, smiling fondly at her. "She has been with you for so long."

"I wish she liked you better," Lyranel murmured, with a glance at her nurse. "She thinks I ought to stick with people of my own rank."

Old Cate shook her head, the long gray braid of her hair bobbing in the firelight. "She only has your best interests at heart, Lyranel."

Lyranel sighed. "I know."

They sat in silence, broken only by the humming of Old Cate's spinning wheel and the crackle of the fire. Lyranel would have to get Paul to bring the old woman some more firewood soon.

She and Nan and Paul had made their way up to Old Cate's cave directly after breakfast, Paul cheerfully hauling the heavy basket of food up the steep path. It was full of broken meats, winter vegetables and pieces of sauce-soaked bread from the first of Christmas' twelve days. Paul had even sneaked in some of Cook's special cakes, so full of dried fruit and nuts that there was hardly room for the rich, dark batter.

Nan had grumbled all the way up the path, but Lyranel knew she didn't really mind. It was pleasant and warm in the cave, even if it did smell of sheep. In the back of the cave, one of Cate's flock bleated softly. Paul had left as soon as they arrived, for he had kitchen chores to attend to.

It was a large cave, with plenty of room for Old Cate and her six woolly friends. She had lived there ever since Lyranel could remember. They called her Old Cate to distinguish her from the town seamstress, Young Cate.

Some time ago, Old Cate's nephew, Edmund, had built a wooden door that fit snugly into the cave's entrance. She and everyone else had to stoop a little to enter her home, but the cave ceiling rose to a comfortable level after that. There was a small hole in the rock above, which let in some light and more importantly, let out smoke from the fire in the pit in the floor below it. Edmund had also laid down a wooden floor for her, and insulated it, so that her feet would be warm.



The cave even had running water, from a small underground spring that never froze even in winter. Edmund, a cooper, had sawn one of his handmade wooden barrels in half and wedged it under the spring to make a drinking trough for the sheep. The other half served as a bed for sickly lambs. Lyranel was thankful that Old Cate's little herd seemed to be doing well. She claimed it was the crisp mountain air that kept them healthy.

Old Cate picked up a handful of clean brushed wool from the basket beside her and worked it into the yarn she was spinning with her long, graceful hands. Her foot pumped the wheel's pedal up and down in a gentle rocking motion.

"Would you like another story?" Old Cate asked.

Lyranel shook her head. She'd already had one treat today. "Yes, but I can't."

"All right," said Old Cate.



Lyranel smiled. As Janissara had suggested, Old Cate could have come to the gatehouse like the townspeople who arrived to receive food and clothing, traditional gifts to the poor on the day after Christmas. The truth was, Lyranel loved going to Old Cate's because of the stories.

She often told them to Lyranel as she made her yarn, the rhythm of her voice speeding or slowing along with her wheel. The old woman could talk for hours, spinning her tales along with her wool. Old Cate's stories were far more interesting than her father's dry old books, of which there were plenty in the castle library. Lyranel didn't mind reading them—the lists of how much wheat was on hand and who had achieved which office and what the armory had been ordered to make always caused images of ancient castle-dwellers to rise in her head. But Cate's stories were better.

Lyranel returned the favor by telling Old Cate about the people in the castle and anything Lyranel found out about other lands. Today, she had told Old Cate about the sickness that seemed to come from Candelo first thing when they had arrived. Old Cate had been fascinated by the news.

"Well," said Lyranel. "I suppose we should go. We have to get back, to get ready for the feast. I wish you could come."



"Me! I'm just an old shepherdess. Why, your father probably wouldn't even let me in the door," said Old Cate.

"He's very generous," said Lyranel. "He wouldn't throw you out. I think."

Old Cate chuckled. "No, no. You go and have your special day, be cosseted and honored by your father and his nobles. I... wouldn't fit in."

"All right." Lyranel rose and gently shook Nan's shoulder. Nan woke with a snort.

"What? Oh. Time to go?" asked Nan.

Lyranel threw on her cloak and led Nan out into the snow. The sun was only now starting its journey towards the west, so they had plenty of time yet to get back. Nan heaved a great sigh at the top of the path.

"I wish you would take your pony," she said.

"I would have to go to the stablemaster, and he would have to go to Father, and then he would ask why I needed Jewel," said Lyranel. "It just seems like an awful amount of trouble."



"But then I, too, would be able to ride," said Nan.

"I'm sorry, Nan."

"Nah, nah. If you can do it, child, then surely so can I. Oh, well, I suppose all this exercise is good for me," she said.

"Yes, otherwise you would be as fat and tender as one of Cook's geese," Lyranel teased.

"Pert child!" said Nan, but she started down the path. She went first, as always. Lyranel had slipped once and the resulting plunge, though not harmful, had terrified them both. Now Nan led the way just in case she had to catch Lyranel.

There were several entrances to the castle, all guarded of course. Duke Trioste was strict about that. Today it was one of her father's many squires on guard duty. The Duke felt it was necessary for someone who was training to be a knight to know what it was like to stand sentry duty. Lyranel knew them all by name. Properly, the guard challenged them as they approached the wooden door. Lyranel approved.

"Advance and be recognized!" he barked, barring the door with his spear.



"The Lady Lyranel and Mistress Nan Bowtham," said Lyranel in a clear, ringing voice.

"Pass," said the squire. Then he smiled. "And a good day to you, Lady Lyranel."

"Thank you, Ferdie," said Lyranel. "Are you coming to the feast tonight?"

Nan snorted her disapproval at this familiarity.

"Alas, no, I shall still be on duty, milady," said Ferdie.

Lyranel nodded and swung past him into the castle, then up the short flight of stairs that led to the second floor and her room.

After the peace of the morning, the afternoon seemed to fly past in a whirlwind of preparation. Lyranel ate a quick lunch, bathed, then went to the chapel for meditation, prayer and a blessing from Father Ignatius. Lyranel liked him. He was homely and young and cheerful, as new to the castle as Janissara, and he always chose her favorite hymns for services.



Alistair then whisked her away for some final coaching in the proper responses to the oath that her father would be asking her to take this evening. She repeated it to Alistair word-perfect. Satisfied, he handed her over to Nan and hurried off to supervise the feast.

Nan helped Lyranel into her favorite overdress, pulling the laces in the back tight and tying them. The gown was a rich blue, made of wool that Cate had spun specially for her. She and Nan elected to keep her hair straight, so as to show off the new diadem. Lyranel tilted her head in the mirror to see it better.

"Careful now," said Nan. "Best not dip your head like that at the feast. We wouldn't want it to slide off into your soup."

Lyranel laughed and sat up straight. "Yes, Nan."

"That's better. Ready?"

Lyranel nodded. With one last glance at the mirror, she reached for her crutches and rose.

The Great Hall, where the feast was to be held, was on the same floor as Lyranel's room. Lyranel slowly walked down the corridor, Nan keeping pace beside her.



They were apparently the last to arrive in the Hall. Lyranel stood in the doorway, peering at a sea of faces. Her father was seated at the High Table on its low dais, where she was to join him after she took the oath. All the nobles, knights, squires and pages who currently lived at the castle were seated at tables, as were the Guildmasters with their journeymen and -women from the town. The provost, the mayor and the shire reeve were there too. Dozens of servants lined the walls, ready to pour and fetch.

Lyranel smiled nervously. It was hard to believe that they were all there for her.

Malcolm, the Duke's Herald, spotted her and pounded a hollow wooden box with the butt of his ceremonial spear three times.

"The Lady Lyranel," Malcolm announced in round, ringing tones. Lyranel smiled in appreciation. Malcolm was a man who knew how to project his voice across the babble of a hundred voices.

As the assembled multitude clapped, Lyranel hobbled across the floor to the High Table and stood before her father. She straightened up as tall as she could, while still leaning on her crutches. Nan took her place just behind and to Lyranel's right.



The Duke, now wearing his gold coronet, rose and walked around the table. He was dressed in a black velvet tunic that came down to his thighs, black leggings and high black leather boots. A gold chain of knighthood was draped across his chest, and he wore his white leather knight's belt as well. Lyranel knew he only dressed this formally for very important occasions. She swallowed as he approached her, her mouth gone suddenly dry.

The Duke stood in front of her and drew his sword out of its worn black suede scabbard. He held it flat in front of her, balanced on his open palms.

Bracing herself on her crutches, Lyranel reached out to place her hands over her father's, with the sword between his palms and hers. She could feel the heat rising from his hands as she pressed her own against the cold metal.

"Lady Lyranel," he said, in a voice that almost rivaled Malcolm's, "you stand before me, your Duke, to take an oath of fealty. If you swear this oath, you will become my representative in all undertakings related to this castle, this town and this land. Are you ready?"



Lyranel licked her lips. "I am," she said, pleased to note that her voice didn't quaver.

"Then so be it. I, Duke Trioste, for my part, take you, Lady Lyranel, to be my sworn vassal, to uphold the law, to succor the helpless and to support and obey me. In return, I will feed, shelter and protect you and yours. Will you in turn, swear to me?"

The oath was very like a knight's, except that she was not required to provide military service.

"I will," said Lyranel, in as strong a voice as she could muster. "I, Lady Lyranel, for my part, swear to be your vassal in all undertakings related to this castle, this town and this land. I will be your representative as your requirements dictate. I will uphold the law, to succor the helpless and to support and obey you, my father and Duke."

As the last words of her oath rang out over the Hall, all of the people there stood and cheered. Applause rose to the high rafters. Against the wall, Paul was grinning and clapping furiously. She could just see Nan's wide smile out of the corner of her eye.

Lyranel's hands were still pressed to the steel of the sword, as were her father's. She glanced at him and was surprised to see that he was smiling. Only a little smile, but it was there.

Her own face split into a grin. Joy bubbled up in her chest. She could feel it wanting to burst out of her—in Song.

She gasped. No! That mustn't happen!

She staggered, her hands flying up, away from her father's sword. She just had time to register the surprise and concern on his face before everything went dark.

# Chapter Four

Nan yanked Lyranel's bed curtains open with a snap, letting in a flood of bright sunlight.

"Up, now," she said. "Long past time for you to be up, I'd say. It's mid-morning already!"

Lyranel groaned and rubbed her sore eyes. They felt as though they were full of grit. She hadn't slept well—again. She hadn't slept well since the day of the feast and that had been almost a week ago.



"Your father missed you at breakfast today," said Nan, frowning.

Lyranel nodded. That was all right. In fact, that was good. The less she saw of him, the better the chance that he would not find her out.

She had barely been able to stifle the Song that had wanted to burst out of her that night, the one that would have doomed her. The effort had been draining. She dimly remembered being carried through the halls after her collapse, but nothing more until morning, when her father had come to ask what had happened.

Nan had suggested that perhaps the stress of the ceremony had caused it and Lyranel did not contradict her, even though her father frowned at the thought. It was far better than the truth.

Ever since then, Lyranel had been terrified that she might accidentally Sing in public, where someone would hear her, and report her to the Duke. But six days had passed without her feeling the urge to Sing again. Maybe… maybe it was going to be all right. She allowed herself to smile a little.



"That's more like it," said Nan. "Such a doleful face you've had this last week. Are you feeling better today, then?"

"I think so," said Lyranel. She threw back the covers, swung her legs over the side of the bed and stretched.

"Hungry?"

To Lyranel's surprise, she was. She'd barely eaten anything all week, out of nervousness. "Yes!"

"That's to the good," said Nan. "Whatever had hold of you must be leaving, then. I wouldn't be surprised if something was wrong with your liver. It wants strengthening."

"I'm sure I'll be fine now, Nan."

"Your father and I were that worried, you know. I was sure he was almost ready to send for–"

"What, Nan?"

"Never you mind, pet," said Nan. She busied herself getting Lyranel's clothing out of the wooden wardrobe next to the bed.

"Did… did Paul go to Old Cate's at all?" asked Lyranel. She hadn't dared to leave her room all week, not even to make the trip up to the cave.

"Oh, aye, that he did," said Nan. "Twice. And I went with him day before last. Even stayed to hear one of those stories of hers."

"You did?" Lyranel asked, startled. "You know that she tells me stories?"

"I'm not always asleep when we are there, you know," Nan said, raising an eyebrow.

"Oh," said Lyranel. She bit her lip. Good thing she hadn't confided her newfound talent to Old Cate then. A very good thing.

"She asked about you," said Nan, laying out Lyranel's clothing on the bed. "Now, off with that chemise, it's time I washed it."

Lyranel's nose wrinkled. True, she had been wearing it all week, either by itself or under her overdress. She wriggled out of it, then into a fresh clean one that Nan handed to her. She slipped the grey wool overdress on over her shoulders, then let it drop to the floor as she stood, holding her bedpost for balance.



"What did you tell Old Cate about me?" Lyranel asked.

"Nought but that you were under the weather. She was tempted to come visit you, but we both agreed that it was unnecessary. I thought you would not want company."

"Thank you, Nan," Lyranel said quietly.

"Off you go to the dining room, now," said Nan, as she bundled up the dirty clothing. "There's some breakfast left for you there. Cold, mind you—you'll have to settle for that."

"That's all right," said Lyranel. "I'm so hungry, I don't care."

"And have you bought your father a Twelfth Night gift yet?"

"Oh! No, I haven't. I meant to," said Lyranel. "But then..."

"Well, that's something you'll have to do today, then," said Nan, "if you're feeling well enough. And Alistair wanted to know if you would be fit to help him plan the Twelfth Night feast."



Lyranel winced. As Lady of the Castle, that was part of her job, too. She'd let him and her father down, moping around and hiding for the last six days.

"Of course," she said. She would have to make it up to both of them—and assure her father that she would be able to do the job he had trusted her with.

After breakfast, Lyranel and Paul made their way up the path to Old Cate's. A heavy snow had fallen the day before, making the rocky path slippery. Lyranel climbed slowly and carefully, Paul behind her with a basket of food from the kitchen.

"You could probably Sing this away, you know," he said.

"What?" said Lyranel, looking over her shoulder.

"I bet it wouldn't be hard," said Paul. "I mean, that first day—when you Sang—it was like spring had come. I felt warm all over."

"You did?"

"Yeah, and happy, too. It's a wonderful thing that you can do, Lyranel."



Lyranel stared at him, then slipped as one crutch skidded on a snow-covered rock.

"But I can't Sing! You know what would happen if Father found out. He'd banish me."

"His own daughter?" asked Paul.

"He might! Please don't tell him," said Lyranel, continuing up the hill.

"Oh, you know I never would."

Paul's mother had brought him to the castle to beg work for him when he was six years old. A few days after he had been assigned to Cook as a replacement for an older boy who had moved on to open up a small inn of his own, Lyranel had found him shivering in a stairwell, homesick and missing his family. Even at four, Lyranel had the idea that a Lord—or a Lady—was someone who took care of the people.

A yell from behind her stopped Lyranel. She swung around in time to see Paul slithering back down the hill, bumping from rock to rock as he scrambled to keep from falling too far. He grabbed at a projecting branch and wrenched himself to a stop just before the edge of the hill. A few items from the basket went tumbling over the cliff.



Paul lay there for a moment, catching his breath. Lyranel started down the path.

"No! Stay there," Paul yelled. "I'll be fine."

He wedged the basket behind a rock and pulled himself up using the branch, wincing as the evergreen needles poked into his hands. Still gripping the branch, he picked up the basket and climbed back up the hill to where Lyranel was waiting, one hand over her mouth.

"Are you all right?" she asked, as he wobbled back onto the path.

"Fine," he said, dusting snow and dirt off his knees. Then he looked at her. "Are you sure you couldn't try even a little Song?" he asked.

Lyranel turned around without a word and began climbing again. She heaved a sigh of relief when the entrance to Old Cate's cave came into view.

"Paul?" the old woman called out. "Is that you? How is—oh!"



Lyranel ducked through the entrance. "Hello," she said.

"Lyranel," said Old Cate, smiling. "I've been worried."

"Yes, Nan told me. I'm... sorry I didn't visit... I've been..."

"That's all right, dear," said Old Cate. "I'm just glad to see you. Come in, come in. And what happened to you?" This was directed at Paul, who was heaving the basket onto her rough table.

"Slipped," was all he said.

"Well, come in and get warm then," said Old Cate. "Oh, look at your hand. Come, let's get those scratches tended."

Paul manfully did not cry out as Old Cate cleaned his wounds and applied a healing balm. "Fetch some rags from my trunk please, Lyranel," she said.

Lyranel hurried to the back of the cave, then returned with bits of torn wool. Old Cate thanked her, then wrapped Paul's hands.

"I think you need some tea after your ordeal," said Old Cate.



"I'll make it," said Lyranel. She knew where Cate kept her tea things and quickly brewed a pot. Paul helped her to fill three mugs, well sweetened with honey.

They settled gratefully around the fire, sipping their tea. Old Cate put her own mug on a small table beside her spinning wheel. Soon, the hum of the wheel and the hot tea had them calmed, even drowsy.

"Would you like a story today?" Old Cate asked.

Lyranel thought there was nothing she would like better, but she still had to go into town and to help Alistair. She opened her mouth to say so, but Paul beat her to it.

"We certainly would," he said. He shrugged when Lyranel looked at him. "Cook gave me leave."

"But..." Lyranel started to say.

"Tell us a story about—about the first Singer," said Paul.

Old Cate's eyebrows rose. "The first Singer? Are you sure?"



Paul's gaze flicked to Lyranel, then back again to Old Cate. "Yes. Please."

"Very well," said Old Cate.

# Chapter Five

"First, did you know that there are actually three types of Singing?" asked Old Cate.

"I know that Singers can alter the world around them, and do healings and that they Sing blessings at events, like births," said Lyranel.

Old Cate's eyebrows rose in surprise. "Now, how in the world did you learn that, down there in the castle?"



Lyranel blushed and Paul grinned. "Listening at corners and keyholes," he said.

"Oh?" said Old Cate.

"It was a game," said Lyranel, with a frown at Paul. "Paul and I used to dare each other. I was eight."

"And I was ten. I recall that I won that day when your father was receiving the Siellan ambassador."

"You only won because father didn't see you cowering behind the door when they left his office," Lyranel retorted, "and we were too terrified to continue on after that."

"I see," said Old Cate, with a bemused smile. "Well, as I was saying, there are different types of Singing. As you seem to know about the first two, I will only add that the third level involves illusion. Singers can make people see things that are not there. It is a kind of hallucination."

"That'd be useful," said Paul. "In a battle, like."

"Yes, indeed," said Old Cate. "Good thought. An interesting one for a simple kitchen boy," she teased.

It was Paul's turn to blush.



"He likes me to read stories about battles and heroes to him," said Lyranel. "They're his favorites. But please go on, Cate."

"Long and long ago," Old Cate began, "before the land had been divided into the present duchies, there was a man named Gavan."

"You mean, before the Compact? When there was still a king?" Paul interrupted.

"Shh," said Lyranel. Old Cate had never told this story before.

"Yes, it was during the time of the Invader Kings," Old Cate said. "Gavan was an ordinary man, a farmer, a man who cared for his land and his animals and always had extraordinary success with his farm. Some said it was luck, some said it was good management—and some said it was because he used a lot of fertilizer."

Lyranel giggled and Paul grinned.

"But I think it was love," said Old Cate. "He was a man who loved the land. He would ride back and forth, watching for pests and parasites, making sure that his fields of wheat had no diseases. Can you see him? Swinging down off his horse, bending down to kneel on one knee, dipping his hand into the rich, dark soil? Bringing it up to his nose, to inhale its musty fragrance?"

Lyranel closed her eyes. A stocky man, wearing homespun clothing and leather boots, with a plain, honest face. A face she could trust. She could see him use a large, but gentle finger to inspect the soil for insects and worms.

Old Cate continued. "He loved his animals too. He made sure that his sheep and pigs and chickens were healthy and thriving. He kept them warm and sheltered and fed them well. The sheep produced so much wool that he kept no less than ten spinsters and two weavers employed all year. His chickens laid so many eggs that he had to give most of them away. Some he gave to a nearby monastery, one that was just being built. His hams and bacons were the finest around and he gave them away, too, along with grain from his fields.

"Then disaster struck. It was a horrible, dry year. No rain fell for months. Gavan's crops drooped for lack of water, and his animals began to wither away. The sun beat down on everything, turning his fertile black soil to gray ash. Then came the grasshoppers. A great wind of them swooped across the land, devouring everything in sight."



Lyranel could almost hear the whir of thousands of wings, clattering faster and faster.

"When they had gone, Gavan's farm was nothing but dust. It was as though the land itself had died," said Old Cate.

She paused, slowing her spinning wheel. Lyranel realized that the noise she had thought was wings was actually the wheel. She looked at Paul to see if he had realized it too, but he was entranced by the story, his mouth slightly open.

"What happened next?" whispered Lyranel.

"Gavan wept. His land, his beautiful land, was destroyed. He went to the monastery, to see if they could help. Their land had been ravaged, too, but along with one lone, thin ewe, they still had the grain and the other foods that Gavan had given them, and so they were able to feed this kind and honest man. But they could do nothing else for him, except pray. So Gavan went back to his farm, and tried to start over. There wasn't much to work with. All he had left were a few seeds and some eggs.

"But Gavan found one thing that gave him hope. As he walked back to his damaged house, he heard a tiny sound. Pulling away some fallen boards, he found that one of his animals had survived. It was a single, solitary lamb.

"Gavan gathered the lamb up in his arms. It was near death, but still breathing. He ran with it in his arms all the way back to the monastery and begged milk for it. The monks shook their heads, because their ewe had not eaten in days and couldn't possibly produce any milk. They allowed him to place the lamb next to the ewe, anyway. Gavan watched, his heart breaking, as neither lamb nor ewe took any notice of the other. Then he opened his mouth—and Sang. To the monks' astonishment, the ewe lifted her head and licked the lamb's ears. Milk flowed from her udder. The lamb struggled to its feet and began to nurse.

"As the little lamb became visibly stronger, Gavan's heart soared. It would live. It would be the start of his new flock. He would remake his farm, as it had been before. Better! He Sang again, this time from pure joy.

"Gavan had become the first Singer and his Song was only the first of many."



Old Cate fell silent and her spinning wheel drifted to a stop. Paul's eyes refocused. He had been deep inside the story, Lyranel knew. He got the same way when she read to him.

"So... can Singers only Sing when they're very sad or happy?" she asked.

"Oh, my, no," said Old Cate. "Any strong emotion will help, but Singers can Sing any time they wish. And sometimes when they don't wish—sometimes they can't help but Sing. Some Singers feel compelled to Sing at sunrise and sunset, too."

Lyranel could see out of the corner of her eye that Paul had given her a quick glance, but she very carefully didn't look at him.

"Singers Sing when there is need," Old Cate added softly.

"Did Gavan's farm recover?" asked Paul.

"Indeed it did," said Old Cate. Her mouth twitched. "You can still see it. Eventually, it became a town named Gavanton."

"Where's that?" asked Paul.



"It's the Singers' town," said Lyranel. "It's on the coast, just at our southern border, the one between Trioste and Siella. They have a school there, where Singers learn to... Sing."

"Yes, they learn to Sing properly, to the best of their abilities," Old Cate agreed. "And other things too. Untrained Singers can hurt themselves and those around them. Most Singers eventually end up there. They are taught the things that Gavan had to learn for himself."

Lyranel bit her lip. Perhaps that was where she would go. The thought was exciting, but scary, too. Despite its chilly stone and faded rugs, the castle was her home.

"But what did Gavan do, exactly?" asked Paul, bringing her back to the present.

Old Cate pumped her wheel again, feeding the wool through her fingers, spinning it into yarn.

"It took Gavan some time to master his Gift. The first time he Sang, he was too busy being happy for the lamb to notice what had happened around him. He didn't see that the apple trees had burst into flower or that the monks' skinny ewe had suddenly become much healthier-looking. The monks, who had been slowly starving to death, found themselves back to their formerly energetic selves. They and Gavan figured out that he had Sung life back into them, at least for a short while."

"Life? From where?" asked Lyranel.

Old Cate shook her head. "The story is old, and does not say. But nevertheless, he found it. Perhaps from the very air around him. After that, his true Singing began. He and the monks planted what little seed they had and kept the few eggs warm. Gavan Sang day and night, encouraging the wheat to grow quickly and the eggs to hatch. He Sang the clouds nearer, so that it rained."

"You can Sing weather?" asked Lyranel.

"Yes," said Cate. "But Singers don't do it very much. It can be dangerous."

"How?" asked Paul. "It would be great to make a sunny day out of a rainy one."

"But what if your land needed that rain? And what if you sent the rain to somewhere that it might cause a flood? That's what almost happened to Gavan. He learned the value of not meddling too much. Most Singers make sure that they don't alter too much around them, or the consequences could be dire."

"Are there Singers who do alter too much?" asked Lyranel.

"Unfortunately, there have been some cases, yes," said Cate, her eyes sad. "They usually destroyed themselves, one way or another."

"Oh," said Lyranel. Maybe it was just as well that she hadn't melted the snow for Paul. She glanced at him, but he was looking intently at Cate.

"What happened to old Gavan, then?" he asked.

"Eventually, he was able to control his Singing, with a lot of work. Surprisingly, he also triggered Singing in some of the monks, and that was quite a shock to their abbot, believe me. But they considered it a gift from God, and the monks later used their talents to help the monastery grow. They studied Singing, and discovered the three levels. The monastery is still there, near the Singers' school, which was built later. There is also a sister house, a nunnery. Gavanton has grown somewhat around them, but they don't mind. It's a beautiful place."



"Have you been there?" asked Lyranel.

"Indeed, yes," said Old Cate, winding some wool around the wheel's spindle. She seemed about to say something, but then smiled at Lyranel instead.

"When did you go?" asked Lyranel.

"I go every year, when I visit my nephew," said Old Cate. "Edmund lives in Gavanton."

"Oh," said Lyranel. "I thought only Singers lived there."

Old Cate chuckled. "Even Singers need barrel-makers. And bakers. And butchers. And seamstresses. Not everyone who lives in Gavanton is a Singer, child. Of course, they mainly sell things to Singers. And it's a seaport, so there are always all sorts of interesting gifts to buy."

"Gifts!" said Lyranel, sitting up straighter. "Oh, Paul, we have to go. I still have to buy father a Twelfth Night gift. And a few others, too." She picked up her crutches and rose. "Thank you for the story, Cate."



"You're welcome, my dears," said Old Cate. "Come back any time. I'm always glad to see you."

"We will," said Lyranel, following Paul out of the cave into the bright sunlight.

# CHAPTER SIX

Lyranel and Paul carefully followed the slippery path back down the hill, but instead of going towards the castle, they took a fork in the path, one that led to the town below. Someone had swept the snow off the cobblestones of the main road, but it was still slippery. They kept to one side, under the overhanging balconies of the houses and shops that lined the street.



It was such a fine day that, despite the cold, many of the merchants had their windows open and their wares displayed on the flat boards that also served as shutters. Lyranel and Paul wandered from shop to shop, peering at the merchandise. There were lots of other people doing the same, probably also looking for Twelfth Night gifts for their friends and relations. Many of them called out greetings to Lyranel.

"Oh, look!" said Lyranel, as they regarded the items displayed in front of a trinket shop. She pointed at several small, carved wooden sheep. "Wouldn't those be lovely for Old Cate?"

Paul grinned. "Perfect."

Lyranel paid for three of them and the merchant wrapped them in fabric.

"What would Nan like, I wonder?" said Lyranel, as she slipped the little package into Paul's empty basket.

Paul shrugged. "No idea."

"I know! More thread for her embroidery," said Lyranel. "We'll go to Threadneedle Street for that."



Threadneedle Street wasn't as busy as the main road. At a small shop specializing in embroidery, Lyranel picked out several lengths of brightly-colored thread, while Paul waited outside. He had very little interest in embroidery and said so.

At another shop, back on the main road, Lyranel pretended to need a rest. She flopped down on a bench just outside a blacksmith's and sent Paul over to a bookseller's across the street to ask if they had any new history books, and then quickly bought a small belt knife for Paul. She managed to hide it in a pocket of her overdress just before he returned.

"No, they haven't any new ones," Paul said as he returned. "Why did you want one? Aren't there enough in the library?"

"Oh, well, I thought father might like another," said Lyranel. "Let's go look anyway. Maybe I'll find something else."

But she didn't. None of the books looked like something her father would like, and the others, she knew he already had. The sun was beginning to slide down towards the horizon when they finally emerged from the shop. Lyranel pulled up the hood of her cloak against the wind that had arisen while they were inside.

"I still have to find something for my father," Lyranel fretted. There were only a few days left before Twelfth Night.

"We could try there," Paul suggested. He pointed to a new stationer's shop across the street. The shop-owner, a woman, was clearing papers and writing implements from her window display, preparing to close for the night.

"I guess so," said Lyranel, "but we'd better hurry."

The woman looked up as they came near and smiled. "Hello. I'm just about to close, dears. Was there anything specific you wanted?"

"I'm looking for something for my father," said Lyranel. "I don't know what he'd like, though."

"What does he do, love? Is he a merchant?" the woman asked.

"No," said Lyranel. "He's the Duke."



"Oh!" said the woman. "Then you'd be Lady Lyranel, wouldn't you?" She shot a rapid glance at Lyranel's crutches.

"Yes, I am."

"And I'm Constance," said the woman, curtseying. "At your service, milady."

"Thank you. Um. . . can you suggest anything?" asked Lyranel.

"Well, I daresay your father probably has enough paper and parchment. Quills? Wax? No? How about one of these, then?" asked Constance.

She held out a finely-crafted long wooden box, with inlaid stained glass decorating its lid.

"It's lovely," said Lyranel. "What is it?"

Constance pulled at one end of the box and the bottom slid out to reveal a drawer divided into sections. "It's a quill case."

"Oh, I see. Yes, that would be lovely gift for my father," said Lyranel. The few times she had seen her father's desk in his office, there had been quills strewn all across it. "I'll take it."



"Certainly," said Constance. "I'll wrap it up for—oh!"

"What?"

"This one's chipped! I never noticed. But that's all right, I have a few more in the back. Do you mind waiting a moment? I'll be quick, I promise."

"That's all right," said Lyranel. Constance disappeared into the back of her shop, and Lyranel glanced down the street. The crowds had thinned considerably since they had arrived in the town. Probably they were all either gone home or heading to an inn for supper. Lyranel's stomach growled. They had a long walk back up to the castle yet before they could have their own.

"Hope she hurries up," said Paul.

There was a crash from within the shop, followed by a yelp.

"What—?" said Lyranel. "Paul, go see if she needs help!"

Paul dropped the basket and leaped over the board and through the window. Lyranel peered into the gloom and saw him disappear around a corner.



She waited, but neither he nor Constance reappeared immediately.

"Is everything all right?" she called out. She couldn't hear an answer, even though she was listening hard. She did hear a faint whimpering.

"Paul?" she said. "Mistress Constance?"

But the whimpering didn't seem to be coming from inside the shop. Lyranel frowned, then hobbled to the side of the shop, where a snow-covered alley led off between the buildings. It seemed deserted. Except for a bundle of tattered fabric mounded up next to the stationery shop, there was nothing there.

Lyranel gasped as the bundle moved. A small bare foot pushed its way out of the fabric, and was quickly withdrawn, back into the dubious warmth of the ragged cloth. Lyranel glanced around, but there was no one else in the alley. The noise could only be coming from whoever was wrapped in the fabric. Lyranel leaned down and gently tugged the fabric away. It was a child. Dirty, with wild, tangled hair half-covering its face. Lyranel thought it might be a boy, but it was hard to tell. There was a wooden begging bowl laid in the snow beside him.

But why was he here? The boy seemed to be about four or five years old. He must have come behind the shop to get out of the wind, Lyranel decided, and then fallen asleep. His parents surely wouldn't have left him in an alley in midwinter, no matter how poor they were. And if he had none, he ought to be in the orphanage. They never turned anyone away; the Duke had made sure of that. Yes, that was where he belonged. Paul could take him there.

Lyranel bent down again and shook the boy's shoulder. He didn't wake. No matter how hard Lyranel shook, his eyes remained closed. Lyranel's gaze fell to the boy's feet and hands, which had fallen out of the tattered cloth. They were white with frostbite. The boy's cheeks were pale too, and he was barely breathing. Even if Paul ran to the orphanage, he might not survive the trip.

Without really thinking about it, Lyranel Sang. The soft, sweet notes poured out of her, in a Song that she almost felt rather than heard. As she watched, the frostbite faded from the boy's hands and feet, leaving healthy pink new skin. The boy sighed, then took a deep breath, and another. Color flooded back into his cheeks. As the notes from Lyranel's Song faded, the boy yawned and sat up, his eyes blinking. He caught sight of Lyranel and smiled.



Lyranel smiled back. Then her eyes widened. Had anyone heard her? The Song had been quiet, but...

She glanced around her wildly, even upwards to the balcony over her head, but no one was in sight. When she looked back, the boy was holding out his begging bowl.

"Alms, milady?" he asked in a high voice.

"C-certainly." Lyranel dug in her belt pouch and dropped a few coins in the bowl.

"Thank you, milady," said the boy. Then he hopped up and scampered down the alley. Lyranel watched him go until he disappeared behind a building.

"Here we are—" came Constance's voice, from around the corner. "Lady Lyranel?"

Lyranel hurried back to the stationery shop. Paul's feet touched ground outside the window as she arrived. "Just saw… something in the alley. What happened? Were you hurt?"

"Oh, that shelf in the back, it's never been too steady," said Constance. "It tipped over. I leaped out of the way, but all my things were scattered over the floor. Thank goodness for your Paul here—he helped me put it all back. Nothing broke. And this was on a different shelf," she added, handing a new case to Lyranel.

Lyranel paid for the wooden box and Paul put it in the basket. Suddenly, Lyranel was tired. They thanked Constance and started to walk up the hill to the castle.

"You were gone when I came back," said Paul. "Where were you?"

"In the alley. I was just… checking on something," said Lyranel.

Lyranel pondered what she had done. She had Sung, just like Gavan, and because of it, a tiny creature had survived.

# Chapter Seven

Lyranel perched on her cushioned window seat above the courtyard and rubbed her aching feet. Despite the cheery fire in the hearth and the thick tapestries on the walls of her room, she was cold. She shivered and wrapped herself more tightly in her woolen cloak. It had snowed heavily in the five days since she and Paul had gone down to the town.

In the courtyard, Paul was carefully navigating the icy cobblestones, a bucket swinging from either hand. Lyranel waved at him through the thick glass. He grinned impudently up at her, then disappeared through the door just below her window. She had missed his company this morning, when she and Nan had climbed the steep path to Old Cate's. He'd been too busy helping in the kitchen. It was Twelfth Night, finally, the last day of the Christmas season.



Nan bustled into Lyranel's room, bringing a draft of the chilly air from the corridor with her. "Here now, let me do that," she said, catching Lyranel in the act of rubbing her feet again.

She nudged a chair closer and propped first one twisted foot and then the other in her lap. Lyranel groaned as Nan massaged and prodded at the tight muscles. Her feet always felt better after Nan had finished, but during, it was akin to torture.

"How's this?" Nan asked, probing at a particularly tender spot. She nodded in satisfaction as Lyranel yelped. "There, I thought that might be sore."

The trail to Old Cate's had been slippery with packed snow. Being careful had made Lyranel's muscles tense. "I had to go," she said.



"I know," said Nan. "The old woman appreciated the food, no doubt."

"She liked my gift, too," said Lyranel. Old Cate had chuckled when she'd opened the fabric wrapper and discovered the carved wooden sheep nestled within.

Nan's hands on her feet were firm but gentle, and already Lyranel's muscles felt less like iron rods and more like human flesh. Nan dug her thumbs into a tight knot up near Lyranel's left knee.

She groaned. "Oh, yes, right there."

Nan nodded and dug deeper. Then she sighed. "Giving charity was something your mother did, too."

"Was it?" asked Lyranel. The thought created a small, warm spot somewhere around her middle. "I'm glad we were able to take Old Cate so much today. Cook was generous."

Nan snorted. "He had nothing to do with it. Paul packed the basket, without Cook's knowledge. Just as well, too. Cook's in a terrible tizzy."

"What is it this time?" asked Lyranel, laughing. Cook had a real name, but no one ever used it. He preferred it that way. He was always in a tizzy over something. Lyranel had never met a fussier fellow.

"It seems someone left the eels out overnight in the courtyard and the water in their tubs froze solid," said Nan. "He doesn't know what they'll taste like once they've thawed. And you can assume that once he finds out who was responsible, life won't be worth living for that individual."

"How can eels taste worse than they already do?" asked Lyranel, wrinkling her nose.

"Eels strengthen your liver," Nan admonished. "You be sure to eat some tonight."

She set Lyranel's feet back on the floor and nudged her thick felt slippers nearer.

Lyranel looked out the window. It was snowing again, big fat flakes that drifted silently to the ground out of the leaden sky.

"So what other dishes does Cook have in mind for tonight's feast?" asked Lyranel.

The feast would likely be even more elaborate than the one they'd had on the first day of Christmas. That had been a solemn occasion, but today there would be entertainment and gifts and merriment, as they celebrated the last day of the old year.



"You've enough curiosity to choke a cat, don't you?" said Nan. "You know Cook; he won't say. He likes his little secrets, he does. Now don't you go trying to pry it out of him. But—I did spot a large bowl of dried rose petals on one of the kitchen tables."

"Rose pudding, do you think?" asked Lyranel. It was one of her favorites. She had helped Paul pick flowers off the Duke's many rose bushes for just that purpose, last summer.

"Perhaps," said Nan. "Or it may be for a subtlety."

Lyranel nodded. Cook liked to surprise Duke Trioste with incredible food sculptures called subtleties. Lyranel wasn't sure why they were called that since they were always spectacular; none of them were in the least bit "subtle." Sometimes they weren't even edible!

"Well, my dear one, eels and rose petals aside, you should be getting ready," said Nan.

"Yes," said Lyranel. "Which should I wear, Nan, the red dress or the green one?"



Nan pursed her lips. "I suppose either of them would be suitable for the season," she said, rising. She skirted Lyranel's bed and reached for the handle of the wooden wardrobe. "But I think I might have something better."

Triumphantly, she swung the door wide. Lyranel gasped as royal blue fabric spilled out, revealing a full-skirted velvet gown with a bodice cut low like a lady's. Wide cloth-of-gold sleeves completed the outfit. It was long enough to cover her unsightly slippers, too.

"Oh, Nan!" said Lyranel. Her hands flew to her mouth.

Nan smiled. "I've had the seamstresses sewing day and night for a week. After all, you will be Lady of the feast tonight, as is your right and duty. It will be good to see someone at the High Table with your father again."

"I'm to be at the High Table?" Lyranel squeaked.

"Of course. You're of age now. Had you forgotten?" Nan asked with a smile.

That meant that she would be in far too close proximity to her father. Her fists clenched. She hadn't tried any more Singing experiments since that time in town. What if, just as at her birthday feast, she couldn't control herself? Lyranel's excitement drained away.



"Your father will meet you outside the Great Hall. You're to go in together," said Nan. "By the way, have you given him his gift yet?"

"No, I was going to give it to him at the feast," said Lyranel. She pointed at her desk, where the carved wooden quill case lay.

"Well, don't forget it, then," said Nan, as she turned away.

Behind her, Lyranel rolled her eyes. Nan still treated her like a child sometimes.

Lyranel balanced on her twisted feet and reached into the wardrobe, pulling the beautiful blue dress off its hanger. The velvet was made of a deep plush and the cloth-of-gold crinkled gently in her hands. It was a point of pride for her to be able to dress herself without help, although sometimes she wished she hadn't made that demand so noisily clear. At least this outfit's outer dress had lacing up the sides to pull it tight, instead of in the back.



When she had it arranged to her satisfaction, Nan dressed her hair, looping strings of the pearls that her father's seaholdings were so famous for through Lyranel's dark russet locks. For a finish, she set the new silver diadem on top and snugged it down to Lyranel's head with pins. Lyranel admired the effect in the tiny mirror, then inspected her face for blemishes. It was hard to tell in the spotted mirror, but she couldn't detect any.

After tucking her father's gift into her belt pouch, she and Nan made their way down the corridor to the Great Hall. Nan went in and Lyranel seated herself on a bench to wait for her father, propping her crutches against the wall, half-hidden behind a tapestry.

The Duke came striding around a corner, speaking earnestly to one of his knights. Sir Thomas, who had property on Trioste's eastern border, saw Lyranel first. His face broke into a wide grin as he registered her presence.

"My Lady!" he said, taking her hand and lightly brushing a kiss across her knuckles. "What a beautiful gown! You are the very image of your mother, blessed be her soul."



"Am I?" said Lyranel. She dimpled, feeling a flush rising in her cheeks.

She glanced at her father. He looked as though he were about to say something, but then his eyes darkened and he looked away. Lyranel wished that Sir Thomas hadn't mentioned her mother.

"Come," said the Duke.

He and Sir Thomas waited while Lyranel retrieved her crutches behind the wall hanging. They courteously kept their pace as slow as her own halting gait. Beyond that first word, the Duke said nothing more.

As Sir Thomas reached for the closed doors of the Great Hall, Lyranel gripped her crutches a little tighter. No matter what, she was determined that she wasn't going to collapse in front of everyone again.

# Chapter Eight

"His Grace, the Duke of Trioste; the Lady Lyranel; and Sir Thomas Riley of Clayborne Mountain Holdfast," Malcolm announced as they entered the Great Hall.

The assembled nobles and other guests rose and clapped. Some faltered as Lyranel hobbled across the floor, no doubt remembering her last appearance there, but they quickly renewed their clapping. The applause continued until all three of them were at the High Table. Sir Thomas helped Lyranel into the high-backed chair next to the Duke, patted her shoulder in a companionable way, and sat on her other side. There were more of her father's knights at the High Table, including doddering old Sir Marcus and his gray-haired Lady Arabella, who sat on the Duke's other side.

"Is your lady wife not attending tonight?" Lyranel asked Sir Thomas, seeing that no one was sharing his plate. Lyranel shared her father's plate. All those not at the High Table used large flat pieces of bread called trenchers, that soaked up the juices of the meats and sauces. They would be given to the poor after the feast.

"No," said Sir Thomas. "Joella is still at home. Our little boy was born only eight days ago, and she is not yet well enough to travel."

"Almost a Christmas baby," said Lyranel. "Like me."

Sir Thomas smiled. "Yes, just like you." He toyed with a spoon on the table.

"Was she troubled by the birth?" Lyranel sipped from her silver wine cup and made a face. The wine, which she usually drank well-watered, was stronger than she had expected.

"No," said Sir Thomas. "It's just that it's a long way to come to the castle, even for a feast such as this. And the babe is not strong, though the midwife tells us that he will be, in time. I only wish…" He stopped, his gaze darting over her head, to where the Duke was absently munching nutmeats from a bowl.

"What?" said Lyranel.

Sir Thomas shook his head. "Nothing."

Lyranel thought she knew what he was going to say. The birth needed a Singing. The boy might yet sicken and die despite all the midwife could do, his little spirit not yet in harmony with its surroundings. A Singer, if one were permitted, could Sing the little one's Song so he could find and hold his place in the web of life. Lyranel almost blurted out to Sir Thomas that she might be able to help. Perhaps if she sneaked out to his home, somehow… but he would be honor-bound to tell her father, and that would be that.

Instead, she asked, "Have you heard about that odd sickness?"



"Yes. I have." He grimaced. "We're rather too close to it, as a matter of fact."

"Has it affected your holdings?" asked Lyranel.

"Not yet, although I have heard of it affecting others who also border Candelo. The mountains are proving no barrier for this, unfortunately."

"Father is sending patrols out to find the source," said Lyranel.

"Yes, and for that we are grateful. I've provided some men for that as well. And dogs."

A commotion at the door to the kitchen drew their attention.

"Oh, look!" said Lyranel.

Cook was strutting towards them. He was leading two men who staggered under the weight of a towering sculpture of bread dough mounted on a long-handled trestle between them. The bread had been baked in the shape of the Duke's crest, a bear rampant, rising on its massive hind legs to paw at the air. The huge animal had been painted black, its nose and claws gold.



Lyranel had no idea how Cook had made the bear look so real, and judging by the reaction of the crowd, neither did anyone else. The Duke applauded enthusiastically. Cook bowed to the High Table, had the men follow him around the Hall to show off his creation, then returned to the kitchen.

The appearance of the subtlety signaled the serving of the first course. Several dishes were brought to the High Table first. Lyranel grimaced when she saw the detested eels, but Cook had provided other dishes as well, including a mushroom pasty and a stew of chicken in rosewater. Lyranel's father heaped some of everything on their shared plate.

Lyranel glanced at Nan, who was talking to a woman seated across from her at the table just below them. Maybe she could get away with not eating any of the eels.

As soon as all the dishes had been served to the other tables, several gaudily-dressed boys and girls burst through the doors and leaped, whooping, into the open space in front of the High Table. Acrobats! Some of them then stood on each other's shoulders, until they were stacked almost as high as the Hall's ceiling. Others twisted themselves into impossible shapes, to the great amusement of the crowd. They gasped and laughed as the tumblers jumped, spun and rolled, seeming to fly through the air, landing with perfect and graceful precision.



"Hhuuu-up!" yelled a tiny blonde girl, who could not have been more than five years old. She cartwheeled down the long stretch of tables, then back again, stopping only when she was back in front of the High Table. She posed while everyone applauded. The Duke tossed her a bag of coins, which she caught and hugged to her small chest.

After a few more flips and rolls, the acrobats all bounded to the back of the Great Hall to sit and eat. Even the entertainers were fed at the Twelfth Night feast.

The dishes were removed by the pages, helped by some of the Duke's younger squires. While everyone ate the second course, a troupe of mummers acted out the story of St. Simeon, who had waited all his life for the Savior to appear and was finally given the gift of seeing Him just before he died.



Cook peeked out from the kitchen, nodded to someone behind him and stepped out. It looked like the third course was going to be preceded by another of Cook's masterpieces. The noise from the throng of feast-goers slowly settled into silence as a large painted wooden crate was trundled into the room on squeaky rollers by the same two men who had carried the bread sculpture. Lyranel peered at the box. She thought she could hear faint snuffling noises.

Then men stopped. Paul emerged from behind the box, scrambled up the side and tugged at the latch on top, then leaped away. All at once, the sides of the box fell outward and slammed to the floor with a series of cracks. Many in the crowd screamed as they saw what the box held.

It was a bear! A live bear!

Safely caged, to be sure, with iron bars all around, but even so! The black bear's long, curved claws were gilded with gold paint, just like the Duke's crest. Lyranel wondered how Cook had managed that.

There wasn't much room in the cage. The bear sat huddled in the far corner, its back pressed up against the bars. Cook was waving his arms and shouting at the bear to stand up. The bear snorted, then turned its back on him. Several people laughed.



"Oh, the poor thing," said Lyranel.

"Who?" asked Sir Thomas, who was grinning at Cook. "Him? Or the beast?"

"The bear," said Lyranel. "It's winter. It should be asleep, shouldn't it?"

Indeed, the animal looked as though it had been rudely awakened. It growled and pawed the air a little.

"I suppose," said Sir Thomas.

The tiny girl acrobat, apparently trying to get a better look, had crept to the front of the Hall and was edging closer to the cage. No one stopped her as she reached out to stroke the animal's black fur through the bars.

But Cook, it seemed, had had enough of the bear's lack of co-operation. He grabbed a long-handled spoon from one of the tables and jabbed the bear with it.

Startled, the bear let out a roar, and stood abruptly. The cage tipped over, and the lid popped off with a clang. Instantly, the bear was out, its huge paws sweeping the air. It connected with Cook, sending him flying across the floor. He lay still, with four parallel scratches in the back of his tunic, oozing blood.

# Chapter Nine

Screams erupted from the audience. The bear growled at Cook, who lay unmoving on the floor, then stood on its hind legs, its front paws high in the air, as if posing for the Duke's crest. Flakes of gold paint swirled in the air, glittering.

With another growl, the bear dropped back to the floor, its paws landing with a double thump. Its great wedge-shaped head swung from side to side. The little girl acrobat screeched in fear as the bear's gaze fastened on her. She scrambled under one of the tables as it paced towards her. Nan and the others seated there screamed and ran, tipping their benches over in their panic to get away.



Lyranel's father fumbled for his sword, but he had not worn it to this peaceful feast. No one here was armed. The best that the Duke had was the knife with which he had cut their meat.

He leaped over the High Table to confront the animal. The bear ignored him, seemingly more interested in the leftover food on the table. Then, without warning, it turned and galloped towards the Duke.

The Duke ran to the door and lunged for Malcolm's ceremonial spear, which he swung around to use as a staff. Lyranel wondered what he planned to do with it. He couldn't herd the animal back to its ruined cage, nor could he let the bear roam through the castle corridors.

One of her father's squires had run up to the upper balcony where the musicians sat. Lyranel didn't know where he had come from. The castle's battlements, perhaps? He was dressed for the outdoors. The squire drew his bow, but hesitated for lack of a clear shot. All the feast-goers were frozen in their places.



The bear rose up on its hind legs once again, pawing the air. The Duke took a step back, then stepped forward once again, making stabbing motions at the bear towering above him. The bear swung one of its hairy arms and batted the flimsy spear out of the Duke's hands.

"Father!" Lyranel screamed. She stood, bracing herself against the table. He drew his knife, but it was pitifully small against the bear's huge claws and yellowed teeth. There was no way that the Duke could stop the animal. If he fought it, he would be hurt, possibly killed! Perhaps if she could distract it—but with what? Something bright and shiny?

Out of desperation, Lyranel reached into her belt pouch and pulled out the quill case that she had planned to give to her father. As the Duke prepared to attack, Lyranel threw the box. It arced upwards, its glass inlay flashing in the light from the torches. It hit the bear, then fell to floor, smashing into tiny pieces. The animal jumped when the box hit it, but kept advancing, its gaze focused on her father.



The bear lunged. There wasn't time to try anything else.

Except…

Lyranel took a deep breath—and Sang. The notes poured out as the Song welled up from somewhere deep within her. It was a soothing Song, full of the quietness of a winter valley; softly-falling snow and the bell-like trickle of an icy stream. The Song urged the bear to be calm, that he was loved and appreciated, and that she knew he was only tired and cranky and wanted to return to his snug, warm cave.

The bear paused. It turned its great head towards her. Lyranel Sang, reaching within herself for the music. She could feel its confusion and anger. Slowly, the bear dropped its paws to the ground, watching her with a puzzled stare. Then it blinked, whuffled, and ambled back to the remains of its cage, where it lay down with a grumbling snort. Lyranels' Song turned softer, into a crooning lullaby. The bear yawned, then closed its eyes and began to snore.

As the last note of Lyranel's Song trailed off, a sigh rippled around the Great Hall. Lyranel let out a sigh of her own and collapsed back into her chair.



The little acrobat girl crept out from under the table, glanced at Lyranel and then back to the sleeping bear. At a particularly loud snore from the animal, she giggled nervously. Whispered conversations broke out all over the Hall. Malcolm cautiously retrieved his shattered spear, then returned to his station at the doors. After a moment, he let someone into the room. Lyranel gave the latecomer a brief glance, but the person was so swathed in layers of clothing that she couldn't make out who it was.

Lyranel sighed again. Her secret was well and truly out now. She was so tired, she didn't really care. Her feet ached, she thought dully.

She glanced at Paul, who was kneeling next to a groggy Cook. He grinned at her and she smiled faintly back. Her gaze traveled to Nan, and despite her exhaustion and worry, Lyranel nearly laughed out loud. Nan was staring at her as if she had sprouted a second head. Lyranel shrugged. Nan closed her mouth and shook her head, her expression grim.



Only then did Lyranel dare to look at her father, the Duke. He was on his knees on the floor of the Great Hall, staring at her. His face was pale. She lifted her chin, steeling herself for his displeasure.

He stood, and staggered toward the High Table.

"You, a Singer?" he whispered. "But how? You have had no training..."

"I don't know how, Father," Lyranel said wearily. "But it's what I am. What I'm meant to be."

It was true. She was a Singer, forbidden or not, whether she wanted to be or not. She knew that now. Nothing could change it, not even her father.

"I'll go pack," said Lyranel.

"What?" said her father.

"The banishment, father. Don't you remember? I have to go."

"Lyranel . . ," her father began.

Lyranel hung her head. "I'm sorry, father. I didn't mean to hurt you."



The Duke swallowed. "You Sing just like your mother did."

"Do I?" Lyranel was startled. "I wish… I had known her. And I wish I knew why you hated her so much," she added, daringly. "Was it because of me? Because of my feet?"

"Hate her?" A great groan escaped from his throat, like that of a wounded animal. "Oh, child, how could you think that?"

Lyranel frowned, puzzled. "But why else would you banish all Singers?"

Her father shook his head. “You don’t understand. I loved your mother with all my soul. I banished Singers because I couldn’t bear to listen to any Songs. They all reminded me of her. Every time I heard one, it was like a spear through my heart.”

“And so you denied the Songs to all!” said a new voice, a woman’s. It was a voice that Lyranel knew, but had not expected to hear. Not in the castle.

“Old Cate?” she said, watching the latecomer unwrap the scarf that had hidden her face. Belying her years, the old woman strode purposefully into the room, then walked behind the High Table to where Lyranel sat. She laid an arm across Lyranel’s shoulders. “Is it really you?”

“Yes, dear one,” she said, grinning. “Oh, Lyranel. I knew there was something different about you that day. I just couldn’t identify it, the more fool I. I have been waiting for this day for ten years.”

Lyranel stared at her. “What do you mean?”

Old Cate’s smile softened. “I was your mother’s Singing teacher, Lyranel. Shortly after she died, I came here, for I thought that some day you might need me.”

"Did you expect me to become a Singer?"

"I hoped you would," said Old Cate. "So did your mother. When you didn't respond to her attempt at healing you, we wondered. Singers are immune to other Singers and their Songs."

"You! I recognize you now. Do you tell me," demanded the Duke, "that I have been sheltering a Singer all this time, despite my decree? Is that why my daughter Sang? Have you been teaching her in secret?"



"No," said Old Cate, quite calmly. "I haven't been teaching Lyranel anything more than the old tales. Which is something Singers need to know, for it is they who pass them on to future generations. Or had you forgotten that? But even if she hadn't turned out to be a Singer, I would not have considered those hours wasted." She turned to Lyranel. "Being a Singer—that Gift comes of itself, when it will."

"I know," said Lyranel, softly. Hers had certainly shown up all by itself.

Old Cate hugged Lyranel, then spoke to the Duke. "And you! Forbidding Singing on your lands! Your Grace, how could you deny that to your people?"

"I had my reasons."

"Tcha! Selfish man," said Cate. "And too proud to lift the ban when you realized what you'd done."

"We prospered," he protested. "No one suffered for the lack of Singing."

"Oh, there was suffering, all right. But not an overwhelming amount, and that only because there were those like myself who were Singing without your knowledge. We kept the land whole, despite your stubborn whim."

"Being stubborn is a good trait in a ruler," said the Duke, lifting his chin in defiance.



"I warned you that you might have to eat your words some day," said Old Cate.

"So did a lot of others," said the Duke, with a grimace. He looked at Lyranel. His voice softened. "I hadn't realized how much I missed the Singing."

"Well, if you are sensible, you won't have to miss it any longer. You can't deny your daughter's Gift," said Old Cate. "Singers need to Sing!"

"I know," said the Duke. "Miriana always said so. But Singers also have to go where they're needed. Miriana died after she was returning from a Singing. I... couldn't bear it, if. . ."

Old Cate snorted. "How could Lyranel go anywhere on these mangled feet? There are others can do the journeying. Lyranel can stay here, and those in need of a Song can come to her."

"But I do need training," said Lyranel. "I don't know enough yet. Won't I have to go to Gavanton?"

"You did very well with that bear," said Old Cate. "But it is true that you still have much to learn, and that an untrained Singer can be dangerous. However, you don't need to go anywhere to find a teacher. I'm right here."



"Oh, Cate! Would you teach me?" Lyranel asked.

"I would be honored," said Old Cate.

Lyranel hugged her, then retrieved her crutches. She glanced around the room. Nan was smiling, with tears running down her round cheeks. Sir Thomas was clapping enthusiastically, as were the other knights and their ladies. Perhaps she could Sing for his son now. Sir Marcus and Lady Arabella beamed genially at everyone.

She looked for Paul too, and finally located him kneeling on the floor near the soundly sleeping bear. He was vainly trying to piece the shattered remains of the little box back together.

"Oh," said Lyranel. She slowly made her way around the table and approached the Duke. "I'm sorry, father. I broke your Twelfth Night gift."

The Duke shook his head and smiled. "It's all right, Lyranel. So. My daughter is a Singer. And I have banished Singers. I will have to do something about that." He raised his head and his voice rang out across the room. "Hear me, people of Trioste. From this day forward, Singers are most welcome on my lands. I hereby lift the banishment. We will have Songs again!"

The people cheered, the noise rising to the high rafters. "All hail Duke Trioste! And his daughter, Lady Lyranel the Singer!"

*End of Book One*

# Book Two

# Journey

# Chapter One

A spring breeze wafted through Lyranel's open window, smelling of flower blossoms and new grass. She could hear Nan singing down below, as she hung bedding on a line in the courtyard. Two bees bumbled by, their striped black and yellow bodies glistening in the sunlight. Lyranel wished she were outside with them.

"Let's try again, dear," said Cate, sitting beside her on the padded bench.



Lyranel turned away from the enticing outdoor scents to face her teacher. So much had changed in the year and a half since that fateful Twelfth Night. Lyranel was still amazed, even after so long, whenever she looked at Cate.

Up in her cave behind the castle, Cate had worn her own homespun wool dresses, her gray hair in a long braid down her back. These days, she dressed more appropriate to her rank. Today she wore a light blue gown of silk over a linen chemise, and a white linen coif covered her hair, which was coiled into a sort of crown on her head. The wide sleeves of the gown were lined with squirrel fur, as were her slippers. Her long, graceful manicured hands lay folded in her lap. Hard to believe that "Old Cate" was actually Lady Caterina of the Singers' Hall.

"Lyranel?" asked Cate. "We need to keep working at this, dear."

"I know," said Lyranel. "It just seems so useless. I'm not getting anywhere!"

"Just try," said Cate.



Lyranel sighed. "All right." She sat up straight and breathed deeply and correctly, starting from her diaphragm, and expanding her chest. She hummed a note with her mouth closed. When she could feel her lips vibrate, she opened her mouth, and Sang.

Lyranel directed her Song at one of the potted crocuses that Paul had brought her earlier in the week. It was a Song of life and water and green-ness. There were no actual words, just the notes and the power behind them. She fancied she could hear the tiny purple flower Singing its own planty little Song back at her, as the crocus turned its trembling petals towards her. As Lyranel ran out of breath, the notes died away.

"So far, so good," said Cate. "Are you ready to take it a little further, now?"

Lyranel nodded, took another breath and Sang again. It seemed to be working. The lavender petals were brightening even as she watched; the stem becoming stronger, the leaves larger. Maybe this time. . . Lyranel Sang louder, intensifying the sound.

The crocus shuddered, then exploded with a *pop*! Shredded stem and flower parts showered both Lyranel and Cate.



"Oh, no," moaned Lyranel.

"Well," said Cate, absently picking bits of stem off her cheek, "you are making progress. The flower lasted a little longer this time."

"I suppose," said Lyranel, as she brushed the shattered petals off her lap.

After the briefest of knocks, a red-cheeked Janissara burst into the room.

"B-begging your pardon… L-lady Lyranel… Lady Caterina," she said, between gulps of air. "His Grace says he requires… your presence. Both of you. Right away."

She was already turning to run down the corridor, when Cate stopped her with a hand on her shoulder. "Where is the Duke?" she asked. "And what's this about?"

"Oh! He is in the Great Hall, milady." Janissara's eyes grew round. "I think someone important is here." Before either of them could ask who, Janissara had pelted back out the door.



"Well," said Cate. "I guess we can continue this later."

With relief, Lyranel gathered up her crutches and rose.

Alistair was waiting for them outside the Great Hall's doors, a worried frown on his normally serene face. Janissara stood at attention beside him, trying to look like she was completely uninterested in anything going on around her, and failing miserably at it. She was still breathing hard.

Lyranel and Cate followed Alistair into the Great Hall. The huge room was empty except for Lyranel's father,

Malcolm the Herald, Father Ignatius, and a group of men and women who all faced the dais. Normally, the dais held the High Table, but today it held only two elaborate high-backed chairs. Her father, dressed in one of his best tunics and wearing his gold ducal coronet, sat in the taller one. The smaller chair beside him was empty. Lyranel gulped. Important guests, indeed, if her father had ordered the ducal thrones brought out. Belatedly, she remembered hearing the sentry's distant horn call earlier in the day, which she had ignored in her concentration on the lessons.



"The Lady Lyranel, Lady of the Castle," Malcolm announced. "Lady Caterina of the Singers' Hall."

Lyranel dipped her head towards her father, then took her place in the smaller throne. A brief frown crossed his face as she passed him. Cate curtseyed, then stood in front of the dais, off to Lyranel's left, beside Alistair and Father Ignatius.

Two men stood in front of the rest of the group on the floor of the Hall. They were dressed more richly than the others, both in robes of parti-colored red and orange, with long dagged sleeves. That was where the similarity ended, however. One of the men was tall and lean, with a clean-shaven face and sleek brown hair showing beneath a complicated hat of folds and coils. The hat's long tail was carefully placed to drape across his chest and fell gracefully to the floor behind him. Lyranel placed him in his mid-twenties. The other man was older, and hugely fat. He wore a ducal coronet, over his thinning gray hair.

"Lyranel," said her father, "this is Duke Candelo. Your Grace, may I present my daughter, Lady Lyranel."

"Charmed," said the older man.



"Welcome to Trioste, Your Grace," said Lyranel.

Duke Candelo cleared his throat, a low rumble, and beckoned with one hand. "Hrrrrm. My brother and Castellan, Evander." The younger man took a brisk step forward.

Lyranel inclined her head. The Duke's brother apparently held a similar position to her own. "We greet you and Sir Evander as guests in our home."

The younger man grinned. "Thank you for the accolade, but it is only Lord Evander, not Sir. I am not a knight."

"Oh. My apologies, my lord." She should have realized that, since he was not wearing a knight's white belt. Which was puzzling; usually members of a Duke's or Duchess's family achieved the rank.

"Apology accepted," said Lord Evander. He had a pleasant tenor voice, she noted.

"Well, hrrrm, now that we've gotten that out of the way," said Duke Candelo, "is there anyplace we can sit and get down to business?"

"Certainly, Candelo," said Lyranel's father. "But shouldn't we see to the disposition of you and your escort first? I assume your guards will be happy to bunk in the castle barracks."



Duke Candelo waved his arm in an expansive gesture. "Hrrrm. To be sure, to be sure. Soldiers are soldiers, eh? They'll sleep anywhere."

"Good. The rest of your party will be lodged in rooms appropriate to their stations," said Duke Trioste. "Lyranel will take care of it."

Lyranel's eyes widened. As Lady of the Castle, this was one of her duties. But she had been so busy with her lessons, that she had hardly had time to pay attention to any of those details. She didn't know which rooms were available for guests.

A flicker of movement from Alistair caught her attention. He stood with both hands behind his back, his fingers moving and intertwining in a way that she recognized. As the Duke's pagemaster, Alistair had invented a kind of language in signs, as a way to communicate with his charges across a crowded, noisy room. Every page started to learn it from the first day. So had Lyranel. She was relieved to find that she hadn't forgotten any of it.



"Lyranel?" her father prodded.

"Yes, father," she said, covertly watching Alistair's hands. "The... west tower room is available for noble guests. Others can be lodged... on the third floor." She looked at Duke Candelo. "Are there any other nobles beside yourself and Lord Evander, Your Grace?"

"Hrrrrm, no, no," said Duke Candelo. "Aside from the guards, t'others are my servants."

Which there seemed to be rather a lot of, thought Lyranel, gazing at the crowd. Only about a dozen of them were in a guard's light armor. "Alistair will find them rooms, also," she said.

"Yes, yes," said Duke Candelo, waving irritably. "Can we get on with it? Been in the saddle all day, you know. Back's killing me."

"Then I won't keep you from a comfortable chair any longer," said Duke Trioste, surprising Lyranel by grinning. "Alistair, see to the accommodations."

"Yes, Your Grace," said Alistair. "Would you like me to arrange for refreshments?"



"Yes, certainly." He rose, nodding. "Please join me in my study, Your Grace. We can talk there."

"As long as it has someplace I can sit," said Duke Candelo. "Like t'get m'boots off, too."

Lyranel's father stepped off the dais and gestured to Duke Candelo and the others to follow him. Two of the servants peeled away from the main group and hurried after them. Malcolm jogged to the doors of the Great Hall, flinging them open just as the small party arrived. They sailed through without faltering.

Meanwhile, Alistair had beckoned to Janissara, who had somehow slipped into the Hall without anyone noticing, and was directing her to take the guards to the barracks. The servants, he took charge of himself. Bowing to Lyranel, he left with them all in train behind him, much like a goose with goslings in tow. Lyranel covered her mouth, stifling a giggle, as she followed her father out of the Hall.

Lyranel's crutches rang on the stone tiles of the corridor. She'd have to get new ones made again; she had grown some in the past couple of months, and this pair was getting too short. Lord Evander, who had fallen into place beside her, glanced down, then quickly up again.



"You have a beautiful castle," he said, smiling. "Very defensible."

"Thank you," said Lyranel. "My father says our ancestors chose the site with that in mind."

"Of course," said Lord Evander.

"Tell me about your castle," said Lyranel.

"My brother's castle, you mean," he said. "It is located at the confluence of two rivers. Our ancestors chose convenience over defensibility, it would seem."

Lyranel's father opened the door to his study and waved them all inside. Duke Candelo made a beeline for the fireplace and plopped into one of the overstuffed leather chairs set near it. One of his servants immediately dropped to one knee and tugged at his master's boots. Duke Candelo groaned as first one boot, then the other, surrendered to the pulling. Lyranel and the others arranged themselves on seats and stools around the room.

There was a tap on the door and Alistair entered, followed by Janissara carrying a tray laden with food, mugs, wine and a clay bottle of cider. Father Ignatius helped her to steady the tray as she laid it on the table in front of the fire. Lyranel's father poured wine into wineglasses and handed them to Cate, Duke Candelo and his brother. Father Ignatius opted for cider, as did Lyranel.



"Well, now, perhaps we can turn to the purpose of your visit," said Lyranel's father.

"Hrmm, yes. Well. The reason I came," said Duke Candelo, "was to talk to your daughter."

# Chapter Two

"M-me?" Lyranel blurted, slopping her cider. "Why?"

"I don't understand," said Lyranel's father.

"Why? Heard this little girl was a powerful Singer, Trioste," said Duke Candelo.

"She is, but..."

"You know about that land plague of ours, a'course."



"Yes. Vierre sent me a letter, which I received near Twelfth Night of last year," said Duke Trioste. "I wondered why I hadn't received one from you."

Duke Candelo's gaze sharpened. "You didn't get mine? I sent it ages ago, as soon as we found the first infestation."

"The mountain pass can be difficult in winter, Candelo," said Lord Evander. "Perhaps the messenger didn't make it."

"Hrrm, yes. What about your lands, Trioste? Any sign of it?"

"Thankfully, we have encountered no instances yet. Sir Thomas and my other knights assure me that our side of the border is quite clear."

"That's good," said Duke Candelo. Then he frowned. "Odd, though. You'd think… well. Never mind. Hrrrm. Earlier this year, the plague patches became more widespread in Candelo. More deadly, too. S'why I need a Singer."



"My brother has an idea that Singers might cure this plague, you see," said Lord Evander.

"Don't you have any Singers in your lands?" asked Lyranel's father.

"We did," said Duke Candelo. "But not lately. Seem to've vanished."

"That's odd. Did you contact the Singers' Hall in Gavanton?" asked Lyranel's father.

"Aye, and they said they'd look into it," said Duke Candelo. "Haven't heard from them since. Maybe it isn't important enough for them."

"Your Grace, my apologies, but I must correct you," said Cate. "I am in regular contact with the Hall, and I know that they find this plague quite important. They have sent several Singers to your lands to investigate."

Lord Evander's head came up. "Truly? Then where are they?"

"Most have returned to Gavanton, exhausted in body and soul. Even the ones who live in Candelo permanently have come seeking sanctuary, saying they could no longer dwell there."



Duke Candelo snorted. "Like rats from a sinking ship."

Cate shook her head. "Something about this plague seems to affect Singers more than most people, Your Grace."

"Hrrrrm. Why was I not told about this?" asked Duke Candelo.

"The Hall did send several messages to you, Your Grace," said Cate.

Duke Candelo's eyes narrowed. "I didn't receive them. As you didn't get mine, Trioste. Hrrrrm. I wonder..."

"You should check it out, Candelo," Lord Evander suggested, his brows drawn down. "Perhaps one of our servants is untrustworthy."

"I will!" said Duke Candelo.

"But what has this to do with my daughter?" asked Lyranel's father, crossing his arms over his chest. "I hope you weren't thinking to talk her into trying to help."

"Hrrrrm! Well, I was," Duke Candelo admitted. "When the Singers' Hall didn't seem interested, I thought I'd come to visit you. Thought your girl might be more inclined to lend her talent to another noble. But if the plague affects Singers..."



"My daughter does not travel," said Lyranel's father.

"In any case, Lyranel is only an apprentice," Cate added. "She does have a strong Gift, but she's still learning."

"Hrrrm. I see. Well, I suppose we may as well continue on to Gavanton, then," said Duke Candelo. He grimaced. "Not that I want to."

"Duke Candelo," said Cate, "I must ask—I mentioned that most Singers had returned to Gavanton, but we are still missing two of them. We were hoping to hear from them soon, but they have not yet returned. Do you know anything about them?"

"Evander?" asked Duke Candelo.

"No. As my brother's Castellan, I have been riding about, checking on the extent of the damage," said Lord Evander. "I have been all over Candelo—but I have heard nothing of any Singers. My sorrow that I cannot give you better news."



Cate sat back, lips compressed into a thin line. "That is very strange. I would give much to know their fate."

"Hrrm. We'll see what we can find," said Duke Candelo. "So. The Singers are concerned. Have you heard anything from them recently?"

"My last letter indicated that no progress has been made, Your Grace," said Cate.

"Blast," said Duke Candelo, wiggling his stocking-clad toes in front of the fire. "Hrrm. Thought you Singers could do anything."

"Unfortunately—or perhaps, fortunately—we have limits," said Cate, smiling a little.

"Hrrm. I understand what you mean. But that doesn't mean I like it," said Duke Candelo. "My people are hurting, and I want to know why!"

"We haven't yet exhausted all of the sources in the Singers' archives," said Cate. "There may be something in the historical records that we simply haven't yet found."

"I'd heard your archives are extensive," said Lord Evander. "Are they open to non-Singers?"



"Yes, as long as you promise to treat them with respect," said Cate. "But I assure you, we have several people searching."

"An extra pair of eyes couldn't hurt. Fresh ones."

"That's true," Cate admitted.

Lord Evander turned to his brother. "Perhaps I should go help, Candelo."

"Good idea!" said Duke Candelo. He let his head fall back against the leather. "Then I would be sure to receive any information you find. And better than that, I won't have to go! Hate traveling, you know. Don't blame your girl for not wanting to go anywhere."

"Mm. Will your brother need an escort?" asked Lyranel's father. "I've had reports of bandits on the roads from my soldiers."

"Thank you, Your Grace, but I think I can take care of myself," said Lord Evander.

"He'll be fine," said Duke Candelo, bending forward to warm his hands at the fire. "Now—I heard this girl put a bear to sleep. A bear! Hard to believe, from such a little slip of a thing."



Lyranel winced. Cate had told her there was already a Song about that incident making the rounds.

"Any way she can Sing for us, Trioste? Like to see for myself," said Duke Candelo.

Lyranel froze. Sing?

"We don't have any bears available for your entertainment, Candelo."

"Ha! No," said Duke Candelo. "But surely, something else...?"

"As I said, Lyranel is only an apprentice," Cate began. "I don't know—"

"I confess I would like to see how well her lessons have progressed thus far," said Lyranel's father. "There must be something she can Sing."

Lyranel swallowed. Her lessons had not been progressing very well at all! She wasn't sure this would be a good time to tell him that, though.

"Your Grace . . ." Cate began.

"Please?" asked the Duke.



"Well," said Cate, clearing her throat, "if Lyranel is to Sing, we must take time to prepare her. By your leave, Your Grace?"

Lyranel's father nodded.

Cate rose and curtsied. Lyranel inclined her head at all of them and followed Cate out the door, which Malcolm held open for them. They didn't speak until they were safely inside Lyranel's room.

"Oh, Cate!" said Lyranel, flopping onto her bed. "I can't Sing! Why didn't I just tell my father that I couldn't?"

"I did suggest it," said Cate.

"I know, I know," said Lyranel. "I didn't want to... tell him I was failing."

"Well... I didn't want to tell him I was failing, either," said Cate.

It wasn't for lack of trying. They had tried several experiments over the months. Paul had volunteered for some of the trials, but after Lyranel had knocked him out cold for an entire day while trying to Sing him to sleep, he had been reluctant to help any more, though he kept quiet about it for her sake. When she had inadvertently caused a blizzard the summer before, Cate had suggested they confine themselves to exercises in control. Lyranel hadn't Sung in public for a year and a half.



"Perhaps you should confess now," said Cate.

"No! Father would be so disappointed with me."

"Well, we know you can control it sometimes. Remember the little boy in the alley? You Sang for him, and he was fine when you were done. In fact, I checked in on him at the orphanage a few days ago. They say he hasn't had so much as a cold since, and is growing like a weed."

"So why can't I do it now?" asked Lyranel, her hands clenching into fists. "Warts!"

Cate shook her head. "After you Sang for the boy, you had to use a strong Song to conquer the bear, especially since it was a large animal and you were untrained. I think that, having learned to 'shout', so to speak, you forgot how to whisper."

"And I can't stop shouting," said Lyranel.

Cate sighed. "Perhaps ten years of being a shepherdess and storyteller instead of a Singer was not such a good idea. I used to be a much better teacher. I wish you could go to Gavanton. There might be someone better equipped to handle you at the Hall."



"Father would never allow it. Oh, Cate, what will I do? If I try to Sing at anything or anyone..." Lyranel shuddered, looking at the sad remains of the poor crocus she had blown apart earlier. She frowned. "Ten years of being a shepherdess... Cate, what if I Sang a story instead? Paul told me he could *see* the stories happening in front of him. And you told me that it was because you were actually Singing them."

"That's because they were illusions. I don't know, Lyranel. Manipulating minds can be more dangerous..."

"*Please*, Cate. I'm sure it will be fine."

"All right," agreed Cate. "All you really have to do is spin a tale in Song. In theory, you would be concentrating on telling the story and so your power would be focused on that."

Lyranel smiled. "So it should work!"

"Let's hope so. Sit up, dear. We don't have much time for you to learn. This type of Singing requires the same technique. But there are differences."



Hours later, Lyranel felt more confident. Her back ached and her mouth felt cottony, but she and Cate had put in a good day's work. She had softly Sung a very short story to a not-so-willing Janissara, and the girl had been entranced. She had even demanded another, but it was then too close to the time that they had to prepare for the evening's feast, hastily planned in honor of their visitors.

Lyranel dressed herself in the same outfit she had worn at Twelfth Night, and had Nan do up her hair with pearls and her silver diadem. The feast, since there were only the two noble visitors, was held in a smaller hall. Six of the Duke's squires were seated at the long table when she and Cate arrived. Several pages stood to attention along the walls, ready to pour wine or water for them all.

Cook had outdone himself, even on such short notice. There were roasted chickens, glazed in a smoky coating; spring vegetables in fragrant sauces; mushroom and onion pasties; and several sweets, including marzipan mice and fruit. No eels, Lyranel was pleased to note. But she couldn't eat much; her stomach clenched every time she thought about what she had to do.



All too soon, the meal was over, and they were all looking at her expectantly.

"Are you ready, Lyranel?" Lyranel's father asked.

"O-of course, Father." She gripped her crutches and stood.

The Song Cate had chosen for her to Sing was the story of how the original Duke Trioste, Duchess Vierre, Duke Candelo and Duchess Siella had rebelled against the last of the terrible Invader Kings and formed the Compact of Four. The line of Invader Kings had for generations overworked both the land and the people, leaving them poor and near death. Sick of the way the people were treated, the four rulers had combined their armies and overthrown Grigori, the last Invader King.

Lyranel concentrated on Singing the story correctly, and on getting the notes just so. Her father and the others sat rapt. It was much the same expression that Janissara had worn earlier. Lyranel glanced at Cate, who smiled at her and nodded. It was working! Feeling confident, Lyranel increased the intensity of the Song as she launched into the final battle scene.



She didn't see how it started, but suddenly plates were flying across the table. Some of the squires had jumped up and were fencing with each other using their table knives. Even Lyranel's father had leaped up to stand on his chair, brandishing his knife at Lord Evander, who was using the marzipan sweets plate as a shield. Duke Candelo was advancing on both of them, knife drawn. It was as if they were acting out the story themselves.

With a gasp, Lyranel stopped Singing. As the last note faded away, everyone else slowly stopped what they were doing, lowering their weapons and frowning at each other as sense regained a hold in their minds. There was one last crash from a thrown bowl.

"That should not have happened," Cate said into the sudden silence, her face white.

Lyranel's father blinked and looked around him, then slowly climbed down and laid his knife carefully on the table. Duke Candelo stared at his knife as if he had never seen it before.



Lord Evander, who had been hiding behind the cake plate, peeked over it at Lyranel.

"Impressive," he said, one eyebrow quirking upwards.

Duke Trioste cleared his throat. "My apologies, my lord. I was not myself."

"No apology needed. Clearly, we were all affected. Your daughter truly is a powerful Singer," said Lord Evander.

"A little too powerful, it seems," said the Duke. "Lyranel, why did you not tell me that your Singing had this… effect?"

"I didn't know that it would, Father," Lyranel said in a very small voice.

It was Cate's turn to clear her throat. "Lyranel has a great Gift, Your Grace. She can perform all aspects of Singing quite exceptionally. She just needs to learn to control it a bit better."

"Control. Yes. I see." Lyranel's father surveyed the room. The squires were watching him closely, not daring to move, even though some of them were trickling blood from various cuts. "Well. I think that concludes our dinner this evening. You may go."



The squires filed out silently, as did the pages. Janissara gave Lyranel a terrified glance.

Duke Candelo was still staring at his knife. He cleared his throat and laid the knife on the table with great care. "Hrrrm. Well, Trioste. Might've started a whole new war, eh?"

Lyranel's father took a breath. "Yes. Perhaps I should have maintained my ban on Singing," he said lightly, with a twisted smile.

"Hrmph! Safer that way, apparently," said Duke Candelo.

"No! Father, I—" Lyranel began, but was cut off.

"Lyranel," said her father, "I'm sorry. You know I didn't mean that. You will just have to work harder at learning to Sing."

"I will, father," said Lyranel. "But not here. I need to go to Gavanton."

"I agree," Cate said softly. "The sooner, the better."

# Chapter Three

Lyranel yawned and poked at the smoky campfire with a long green stick. It looked like it was going to be a nicer day for traveling than the previous one, which had been gray and drizzly. Yesterday, they had ridden through patchy rain showers until it had started to get dark in earnest and they decided to stop for the night. Paul and the others had not been happy about pitching their tents in the rain.

"They will be wet inside and smell besides," Nan had protested. "Could we not stay at an inn?"

But there had been none close by when they decided that they had to stop, and Cate had thought it best that Lyranel not be surrounded by strangers anyway. Lyranel had accepted that with relief. Cate, to mollify Nan, had Sung the moisture out of the tents, leaving the insides clean and dry. Nan had pretended to still be annoyed, but Lyranel could tell she had been pleased.

For all their hurry to be on their way to Gavanton, what with one thing and another, it had been two weeks before they could set out. Upon hearing of the upcoming trip, Nan had insisted that Lyranel needed to prepare and pack properly for a stay at the Singers' Hall. They had also needed to organize supplies for the four-day ride for several people. And Nan wouldn't hear of Lyranel going alone, with no maid to look after her, so she had added herself to the group.

Lyranel's father had tried to argue Lyranel out of the trip, reminding her of her oath and duties as Lady of the Castle. But she had held firm, with Cate's support.



"I almost caused a war, Father!" she had cried. "What if something worse happens?"

He hadn't been able to answer that, and he refrained from more comments. In fact, Lyranel barely saw him at all after that. He was gone before breakfast and returned after the supper hour—out riding, inspecting the lands, Alistair said. There had been rumors of the land plague appearing here and there on the border. Lord Evander had gone with him a time or two and had even ridden out by himself once, when the Duke was busy.

With his brother having gone back to Candelo, Lord Evander had elected to delay his own journey so that he could accompany them. Lyranel wasn't sure she wanted him to—his presence reminded her of her embarrassment—but it made sense for them to all travel together. Lyranel's father had said that he had too much work to do to go with them to Gavanton and arranged for guards instead. Cook had reluctantly let Paul go, calling him his "best boy," which made Paul blush all the way to the roots of his fair hair. Lyranel had grinned behind her hand at that.



After Father Ignatius had blessed their journey, they had left. Lyranel's father had ridden with them through the town below the castle, stiff and silent in his saddle. At the town's edge, he had hugged Lyranel briefly, wished them a good trip and then cantered away across the fields without a backward glance.

That had been three days ago. Lyranel poked at the fire again. A piece of charred wood flipped over, showing the glowing red ember inside. Cate emerged from the woods and came to sit on a stump beside her. Despite the rough conditions, she always looked the perfect lady, as if she had just come from a session with maid and hairdresser, though Lyranel knew that she had refused Nan's offer of help. Lyranel didn't know how she did it. Perhaps it came from living alone all those years.

"Have you Sung the sun up?" asked Lyranel.

"Yes, indeed," said Cate. There was a calm serenity about her that Lyranel envied.

"I wish I could help you do that," she said. She felt the tug herself every morning, but hadn't dared to try in case something awful happened. "I always feel I should."



"I wish you could too," said Cate. "Why don't you try?"

Lyranel shook her head. "I'm afraid to."

"Well, the sun rises and sets whether we Sing or not," said Cate. "The Morning Song is simply a way of preparing ourselves for the day. I find it calming and energizing at the same time. And at sunset, the EvenSong tells us to lay down our busy-ness and rest." She grinned. "I Sang both every day in my cave, you know. Just very, very quietly."

"My father would not be pleased to know that," said Lyranel, grinning back.

"Sometimes I think I'd like to still be there," said Cate. "Life was simpler then. And I miss my sheep."

Cate's little flock was now tended by a young couple who had taken over her cave, trying to make a living off the land.

"Me, too," said Lyranel. "I wish you could have told me that you were a Singer then."

"I couldn't, darling. Not that you would have told anyone, I know. But I couldn't reveal myself. Your father might have found out."



"I know." Lyranel sighed, smacking a coal with her stick. It bounced up and landed near her foot.

"Something wrong?" asked Cate.

"My father… when we left, he was so…"

"He loves you very much, Lyranel," said Cate. "It is hard on him to see you go. Remember, your mother rode away from him too, and then never came back."

Lyranel nodded. "I know. I just wish he would tell me."

"He was always a very private man," said Cate. "He showed his love in deeds, not words. He loved your mother. She knew it, though he never told her."

"I don't remember my mother much," said Lyranel. "Was she a strong Singer, too?"

"Oh, yes," said Cate. "She had a great affinity for growing things—like Gavan. If an animal needed her, she knew it without even being told. Even if they were far away, sometimes."



"Did I get my strength from her, then?" asked Lyranel.

"Probably, although it is not necessarily passed down from parent to child," said Cate. "Sometimes it happens, and sometimes it doesn't. There are Singers with non-Singing children, and certainly plenty of ordinary people who have been surprised out of their wits by their child suddenly developing the talent."

"There are also lots of children who always wanted to be Singers," said Paul, handing Lyranel and Cate each a mug of steaming tea.

"Like you?" Lyranel teased. "When we were little, you told me you wanted more than anything to be a knight. You didn't say anything about being a Singer."

"Ever since you first Sang on Saint Stephen's Day, I kept hoping," said Paul. He shrugged. "I don't have a chance of becoming a knight, but I might have become a Singer. Others like me have. But I guess I'll just have to be happy to be a master cook some day."

He turned away and knelt by the fire to prop a four-legged flat griddle over the coals. A moment later, he ladled a thick oatmeal paste over the hot metal. A delicious smell of cinnamon and raisins wafted upwards as the oat cakes sizzled. Paul waited, then deftly flipped them just as they were turning a golden brown on the bottom.

Nan and Lord Evander joined them just as the cakes were ready to eat. Nan was laughing at something that Lord Evander said. He had flirted with her outrageously on the road the day before, leaving Lyranel's nurse giggling like a young girl.

"Lady Caterina, are we ready to go?" asked Nan, once they had all finished their breakfast. Nan's opinion of

Cate had risen, ever since she had found out that Cate was not a simple shepherdess.

The two men-at-arms that the Duke had assigned to be their escort had already packed up the tents and bedrolls. Nan had wanted to take a wagon and travel in style, but both Cate and Lyranel had vetoed that, preferring to travel light. Lord Evander rose and made his way to where the horses were tethered. He laughed at something that Fergus, one of the Duke's men-at-arms, said and slapped his shoulder.



"Do you think we'll reach Gavanton today?" Lyranel asked Cate.

"We might if we travel through the night as well as the day," said Cate. "That wouldn't be a problem, though. The Hall is used to Singers draggling in at all hours. There is always someone serving as porter, no matter the time."

"Given the weather, we will probably meet more people on the road today. That could slow us down," said Paul.

"Yes," Cate agreed. "And we will encounter more as we get closer to the city."

Yesterday, they had only met a few people, this deep in the Firwood Forest. A family on a wagon had gone by them, heading in the opposite direction, the children waving madly from underneath the tarpaulin. Some merchants had passed by as well—one of them had ridden alongside them for a time, talking with Lord Evander and Nan, before galloping off down the road. There had also been a troop of the Duke's soldiers. Their female commander had stopped to talk with Fergus, saying something about rumors of bandits and warned them to keep an eye out for the land plague. They had saluted Lyranel as they rode past, on their way to report to her father.



Lyranel handed her mug and bowl to Paul, then reached for her crutches and rose, heading towards the horses.

"May I help you?" Lord Evander said from behind her.

"No, thank you," she said. "I'm fine."

"Are you sure?"

Lyranel didn't answer. Her horse, Diamond, was taller than Jewel, and for a brief moment she wished she had brought the smaller animal. But she knew that Jewel would not have fared as well on the long trip. Better to have the sturdier, long-legged mare, who was a beauty of a golden horse with a white diamond on her shapely forehead. Lyranel had used a mounting block at the castle, but here there were no such conveniences. But she knew what to do. She slid her crutches through the straps that held them tied to the saddle, then grasped the pommel in one hand and the cantle in the other.



Her arms, from years of walking with crutches, were the strongest part of her body. With a little hop, Lyranel pulled herself up until she could slip one foot into the stirrup, then swung her other leg over. She settled the folds of her split-skirt riding outfit and slipped her other foot into the opposite stirrup.

"You see?" she said.

Lord Evander's mouth twitched. "My apologies, Lady Lyranel."

They were soon on their way, heading west at a steady walk. The road was drying from the previous day's rain, but there were still puddles in the wagon ruts. The horses plodded on, oblivious to the mud that spattered up their legs. Toby and Paul were bringing up the rear today. Lyranel glanced back at them just in time to see Paul double over laughing at something the younger man-at-arms had said.

Nan slowed her horse so that she was riding beside Lyranel. Cate did as well, riding on Lyranel's other side.

"That Lord Evander is such a nice fellow," said Nan, watching him talk with Fergus, up ahead. "He says the most outrageous things."

"He's all right," said Lyranel. She turned to Cate. "Why isn't he a knight, though? He ought to be, being a Duke's brother. Do you know?"



Cate tipped her head to one side. "Not really, no. I'd heard a rumor that it was because he had done something unchivalric when he was just a boy. The Duke punished him by refusing to make him a knight. Apparently, he hasn't yet changed his mind. Silly. All boys do unchivalric things. They usually grow out of them."

They rode in silence for a few minutes.

"I wonder if we'll meet any more merchants today," said Nan. "That fellow who rode with us for a time yesterday said there's a fair going on in Gavanton, a big wool and fabric fair, and that we'd do well to get there early. I told him I hoped there would be embroidery thread as well. I need some red."

Cate frowned. "A fair? I don't know of any Gavanton fairs at this time of year."

"Perhaps it's new," said Nan, shrugging.

"I suppose," said Cate. "What kind of merchant was he?"

"He said he was a wool merchant," said Nan.



"Really? Odd," said Cate. "I thought I knew all the wool merchants hereabouts. . ."

"Maybe he's from another duchy," Lyranel suggested.

A flock of small black birds suddenly took flight from one side of the road, rising up from the dense forest.

"He could be—" Cate began, but she was interrupted by a cry of pain from the front of their column. "What . . ?"

An arrow protruded from Fergus's arm. Before Lyranel could register what that meant, there was a sudden thrashing in the brush, and a dozen men and women leaped out of the forest to stand in front of them on the road. Some of them aimed drawn bows at their little group. The rest of them brandished axes or long knives.

"Bandits!" Lord Evander shouted.

There were too many to fight. Lyranel yanked on Diamond's reins to turn the mare around. But there were already more bandits behind them. Paul struggled in the grip of a man who had pulled him from his saddle. Fergus was face down on the ground, not moving, bleeding sluggishly from his wound. Toby was grappling with another bandit, this one wielding an axe. Lyranel gasped as the axe flashed down.



"Get her!" a man yelled.

She kicked at a hand that was reaching for her ankle, and was rewarded by a yelp. Did she dare Sing? Causing this bunch to fight among themselves might be a good thing. But what if Paul or the others got hurt? She'd have to chance it.

She let the notes pour out in an explosion of sound. Diamond screamed and reared, and Lyranel was thrown from her back. She landed on the ground with a grunt, the breath knocked out of her. Someone grabbed her from behind and slapped a rough hand over her mouth. Lyranel tasted sweat and dirt as she bit down. Her captor swore. Then pain exploded behind her right ear, sending stars across her vision.

Her last sight before everything went black was of one of the bandits swinging his axe at Cate.

# Chapter Four

◇◇◇◇◇◇◇◇◇◇◇◇◇◇◇◇◇◇◇◇◇◇◇◇◇◇◇◇◇◇◇◇◇◇◇◇◇◇◇◇◇◇◇◇◇◇◇◇◇◇◇◇◇◇◇

The world swam slowly back into focus. Lyranel tried to open her eyes and saw only darkness. Was it night? No, she was looking up into the tangled branches of trees, so tightly grown together that they shut out most of the light.

"Owww," said Lyranel. Her head hurt.

"Lady Lyranel?" someone asked.

"Who . . ?" said Lyranel. She squinted, trying to locate the source of the voice. She turned her head, wincing as pain stabbed somewhere behind her eyes. Her stomach churned.

"It's me. Evander," he said. He was sitting beside her, his back against the tree. She couldn't see his face properly. "Are you all right?"

Lyranel blinked. "I think so. Except for the headache."

"Thanks be. I was worried," said Lord Evander.

"What… happened?" asked Lyranel.

"We were ambushed."

Oh, yes. Now she remembered. She struggled to sit up. Like Lord Evander's, her hands and feet were bound with rough rope. She tugged at them, but it was no use. Maybe she could Sing them off? No, she would probably cause them to burst into flame. She gave up, lying back down and letting her head drop to the forest floor.

"Ouch!" she cried.

"Sore?" asked Lord Evander. "I'm not surprised. You were knocked out." He made a disgusted noise. "So was I. One of the bandits took the flat of an axe to the side of my head. Then they disarmed me. At least we weren't killed. I guess they must have realized that you and I were the only valuable ones. No doubt they will try to ransom us."



Lyranel lifted her arms and tried to touch the bump on the back of her head, but couldn't reach far enough. "Killed? Oh, I almost wish I had been. My head hurts."

"Don't think it, Lady Lyranel. We were the lucky ones."

"The lucky ones? What do you mean?" asked Lyranel. She looked around. "Where is everyone else?"

Lord Evander didn't answer.

"Were they killed?" Lyranel whispered.

"We can't do anything for them, Lady Lyranel." Lord Evander turned his head away from her.

Nan, Cate, Paul—dead? How could it be? They were all alive just a little while ago. It just didn't seem possible that she would never see them again. Never to feel Nan's arms around her or hear Cate Sing? Or see Paul? Tears leaked down Lyranel's face, dripping into the loam beneath the trees. She sniffled, then wiped her face on her sleeve.

"All right then," said a gruff voice. "Time to go, me precious cargo."



Lyranel lifted her head, ignoring the stab of pain that accompanied the motion, to look into a dirt-smeared face, half-hidden by a raised hood. One of the bandits! She tried to scrunch closer to the tree.

"Go where?" asked Lord Evander.

"To our palatial hideout, princeling," said the bandit. A long red braid slipped out from under the hood.

"Why, you're a woman!" said Lyranel.

The bandit let her hood fall back on her shoulders. She was tall and rangy, dressed in a man's leather breeches and a wool shirt. "So I am, lovey. What, did you think bandits were all men? Even women have to survive. Now, up you come." She pulled on Lyranel's bound arms.

Lyranel struggled to stand, but it wasn't possible. "My feet," she cried. "I can't walk."

"Why not?" The woman peered at Lyranel, frowning.

"I was born with clubfoot," said Lyranel. "My ankles were broken when I was a baby. So I can't walk."



"I don't know how we'll get you where we need to go, if you can't keep up."

"I can keep up just fine," said Lyranel. "Just give me my crutches, and I'll show you. They're on my horse."

"Sorry, sweetie, no crutches. No horse!"

"What happened to Diamond?"

The woman shrugged. "Diamond, is it? Pretty name. Ah, somewhere off in the bush, I suppose. She kicked one of my men and galloped away. Fast, that one. Mighta had something to do with that old woman's caterwauling. What a racket! I wish I could send a couple of my men to look for the animal—fine horseflesh like that ain't easy to come by."

"Your men?" asked Lyranel. "Are you the... leader?"

"And what if I am?" the woman asked, one fist on her hip. "I earned it fair and square."

"Oh," said Lyranel. "I'm sure you did. Well, whatever ransom you are asking, my father will pay it. I know he will."

The woman chuckled. "I'm sure he will, little one. Meanwhile, you come with us. I guess you could ride behind me."



"What about me?" asked Lord Evander.

"You can walk," said the woman, mounting a waiting horse. She beckoned to one of her men, who cut the ropes that bound Lyranel's hands and feet, then hoisted her roughly into the saddle. Blood rushed painfully into her numb fingers.

"There you go, Mhaire," said the man. "Now you hold on tight to her belt, girl. That's it. Now you." He attached a short line to the bonds on Lord Evander's wrists, then loosened the ones around his ankles. Lord Evander was still bound, but he could walk like a hobbled horse. The man attached the short line to the saddle of another horse and pulled Lord Evander to his feet.

"Move out!" Mhaire shouted. Her horse jounced along at a brisk walk through the trees, heading south and east, away from the main road. Lyranel felt ill, but she was not going to give these bandits the satisfaction of watching her throw up. Instead, she concentrated on sitting as tall as possible. She would show them she was a lady.

Much later, she woke to find herself leaning against Mhaire's back. The woman had tucked Lyranel's hands into her broad belt to keep her from falling. She wriggled them out and sat straight again.



"Back with us, are you?" asked Mhaire. "We're here."

Lyranel looked around. They were in a clearing, deep in the woods. Several people came running towards them, from huts made of twigs and branches that blended into the surrounding trees. Two small fires were burning, one of them tended by a tall girl with a messy blonde braid down her back. She was watching a cauldron that was suspended high above the fire on a metal tripod.

"Time for you to get off," said Mhaire.

"I-I can't," said Lyranel.

"Oh, the feet," said Mhaire. "Oy! Conn! Come and help her ladyship here."

The same man who had helped Lyranel to mount Mhaire's horse jogged cheerfully closer.

"Down you come then, girl," he said. Lyranel half-slid, half-fell off the horse into Conn's waiting arms. "There you go. Now lean on me and we'll get you settled."

Lyranel staggered beside him, held up by one of his arms. She didn't want to touch his filthy, ragged clothing, but she had no choice. She hadn't had to put all of her weight on her feet since her first pair of crutches. They passed out of direct sunlight into the gloom under the trees. Lyranel kept a close eye on the ground to make sure she didn't stumble over anything.



"What's wrong with her, Da?" someone asked. Lyranel looked up into the smudged face of the girl who had been tending the fire.

"Her feet don't work, Elsie," said Conn.

Elsie snorted. "Huh. Why'n't you leave her behind, then?"

"She's valuable," said Conn. "Now mind your own business. Looks like your pot's boiling over."

"Cow plop!" said Elsie, scurrying back to the fire.

Lyranel's chest was heaving from her unaccustomed attempt at walking by the time Conn got her to a nearby tree. She slid down to rest on the springy loam underneath, breathing in ragged gasps.



Conn shook his head and scratched at his neck as he watched her. "Well, now, don't know what we're going to do with you, for all that. Ah, well, not mine to worry about." He walked towards the fire and sniffed at the pot.

Elsie glanced at Lyranel and sneered. She pretended to stagger and leaned heavily on her father. "Help me, Da! I can't walk!"

He laughed and elbowed her away. Then he grabbed her and hugged her close, tucking her head under his arm. Elsie squawked and punched at his back with her fists.

Lyranel was still breathing hard. Her ankles ached, and the entire length of her legs was trembling. She tried to think of some of the calming exercises that Cate had taught her. Fresh tears started in her eyes at the memory of her teacher. Gritting her teeth, she shook them away and wiped her sweaty face on her cloak.

Lord Evander, she saw, was tied securely to a tree halfway around the clearing from hers, his arms and legs still bound. Conn hadn't bothered to tie Lyranel up again, likely trusting to her inability to walk to keep her from escaping. As she leaned her head wearily against the tree trunk, she had to admit that he was right on that score. Her whole body ached and she was too tired even to think straight. She closed her eyes, just for a moment.

# Chapter Five

When Lyranel woke again, it really was dark. She licked dry, cracked lips and blinked several times. It was frustrating, this tendency of hers to fall asleep. She hoped it would stop soon. Perhaps it was because of the lump that the bandit had given her. Her head still throbbed.

Torches and firelight flickered in the clearing, shining on the bandits going to and fro on mysterious errands. The girl, Elsie, was no longer tending the big cauldron, which had been lifted off the fire and was sitting in the dirt on its three sturdy legs.



"Oh, so you're awake again, are you?" asked a familiar voice. It was Elsie, leaning against a nearby tree. She picked pieces of something out of a wooden bowl and chewed as she watched Lyranel.

"Please, may I have something to eat?" asked Lyranel. Her stomach was still queasy, but she hadn't eaten anything since Paul's excellent breakfast and that had been a very long time ago.

Elsie tilted the bowl towards her lips and slurped up the last of her meal, as if she hadn't heard Lyranel. Lyranel was about to ask again, when Elsie thrust herself away from her tree and flounced over to the cauldron. She dipped the bowl into it and brought the bowl back to Lyranel.

"Thank you," said Lyranel, as Elsie handed her the bowl. Lyranel took a sniff and recoiled. The stew was thick with roots and bits of meat, but it was greasy and burnt.

"Too proud to eat my ma's stew?" asked Elsie.



Lyranel grimaced. Paul would have made a much better one. She wondered what the meat was—rabbit perhaps, or squirrel. Or something less reputable. She was too hungry to care, though.

"Huh," Elsie snorted, as Lyranel downed the whole mess. "You wanting more, then? Well, you can't have it. We can't afford to feed someone who doesn't pull her own weight."

"But I'm still hungry," said Lyranel.

"But I'm still hungry," Elsie mocked. "Oh, you poor thing. I bet you never missed a meal in your life. Have you ever had to go for three days without food in your belly? I have. You have no idea what 'hungry' is."

"No," said Lyranel. "I suppose I don't. I've lived in a castle all my life."

"Ooh, a castle! Well, lah-di-dah. The high life. A place where even people who can't walk are allowed to live," said Elsie. "Your parents should have left you for the wolves. That's what I'da done if you was my get."

"What?" said Lyranel. "Why?"

Elsie spat. "Don't know much about bein' poor, do you? In my world, someone like you wouldn't survive. In fact, if it was mine to say, I'd kill you now and get it over with. But Da says you're valuable." She grinned. "Bet we're going to sell you to some slave-owner. That's what we usually do with folks like you."

"Y-you do?" asked Lyranel. "B-but my father will pay a ransom."

Elsie laughed. "Ransom, eh? Don't get your hopes up." She grabbed the bowl from Lyranel and stalked away.

Lyranel looked for Lord Evander. He was still tied to the same tree, although someone had loosened his bonds so that he could eat. He'd said the bandits would only want to be paid. But how could he prevent it, if they truly wanted to make money on them some other way?

Most of the bandits were lounging around the clearing, their backs against trees, or sitting on stumps around the fire. Mhaire was sitting on a log, conversing with one of her men. One of them began to sing a folk song, about traveling the valleys and the high roads. It wasn't Singing, but it was pleasant, and he had a nice voice. Lyranel found herself caught up in it. When he was done, another bandit, a woman this time, sang a love song, about two people unable to love and marry as they chose.



"Who's next?" someone called, when she was finished. "Elsie? Give us a song?"

"Nah, not tonight," said Elsie.

"Come on, Elsie," said her father. "You always do."

"Oh, all right," said Elsie. She stood and, to Lyranel's astonishment, Sang!

The Song was rough and unfocussed, for Elsie had not prepared herself properly and neither did she breathe the way that Lyranel had been taught, but for all that, it was definitely a Song. Lyranel listened critically to the tale she spun about a bandit king and how he championed the poor.

All the bandits clapped when she finished. "How about another?" someone called out.

Elsie, who had sat down near the fire, shook her head. "Not tonight, Hamish. I'm all worn out with tending Mistress Useless over there." She pointed at Lyranel.

Lyranel's eyes narrowed. Useless! She'd show them. If they wanted Singing, she'd give them real Singing. She didn't care if they ended up fighting among themselves.

Lyranel straightened as much as she could and, taking a proper breath, she opened her mouth. As the first few strong notes floated up into the sky like sparks from the fire, several of the bandits turned to look at her. Lyranel Sang a story of a great king and his knights, a legend of long ago. She threw herself into it, and Sang of how the king defeated his enemies, only to be brought down by treachery from the people he trusted most. Her Song wrapped the bandits in an illusion of seeing the story unfold before them.

A part of her marveled that she was actually Singing, and nothing bad was happening. She let the Song trail off quietly, puzzled.

There was a respectful silence. Then someone said, "Thank you, Lady."

Lyranel looked up, into Elsie's wondering eyes. A sweet smile curved her lips, making her look almost pretty. Then she shook her head abruptly and glared at Lyranel.

"Better than you, eh, Elsie?" called Hamish.



Elsie lurched upright and stomped off into the trees. Someone chuckled.

"Would you Sing us another one, Lady?" asked Conn. "No one told us you was a Singer too."

"I can't," Lyranel croaked from a throat gone dry.

"I'll get you some water!" said Hamish, leaping up and running to a barrel. He dipped a ladle in and brought it to Lyranel. She drank gratefully. The water, unlike the stew, was sweet and clean on her tongue.

"Now can you Sing again?" Hamish asked.

Lyranel nodded. What to Sing next? Cate had promised to tell her some new stories, but she hadn't had time before... Lyranel swallowed the lump that threatened to form in her throat.

She wished Cate were here, to see her Singing properly. How was she doing it?

Perhaps it was the size of the group that was the key. It took all of her ability to spin the illusions for so many people.

They were waiting for her, politely. Even bandits could be courteous when they were listening to a Singer, she supposed. Lyranel Sang again, this time a love song like the one the woman had sung, except Lyranel's had a happy ending. Once again, she had no problem. The bandits smiled and clapped and asked for another. Lyranel took another drink of water, then launched into a slow Song, one that was popular on the sea coast, about sailing in the wide ocean, never knowing if the sea would let you come home to your family again.

The rhythm of that one was soothing and many of the bandits laid back on the ground, or relaxed against their trees as she Sang. An idea swirled in her mind. Maybe... she subtly altered the Song's rhythm to one that was closer to the Song she had Sung to the bear. It was a lullaby, meant to soothe, urging all the listeners to relax, to rest, and finally, to sleep. She hoped it would also knock out any unfriendly animals that happened to be lurking.

When she finished, Lyranel looked around her. All of the bandits were deep in slumber, slumped on the ground or against trees. Some were even snoring.

Lyranel staggered to her feet, holding on to her tree for support. She and Lord Evander could escape now, so that the bandits couldn't sell them to any slave-owners. They would probably all sleep for hours, thanks to the power of her Song, as long as nothing woke them. At least that was what she had intended. Without crutches, it would take her a very long time to get away from them, and to find someone who might be able to send word to her father. They might go a little faster if Lord Evander carried her.

She looked for him, then grimaced. Lord Evander was asleep too. She would have to make her slow way around the edge of the camp to wake him. She didn't dare try yelling or Singing.

Lyranel turned around, and rocked back, almost losing her balance. Elsie was standing there, staring at her out of wide eyes.

"How did you do that?" the bandit girl whispered.

# Chapter Six

Lyranel groaned. She'd forgotten that, as a Singer—even a weak one—Elsie would be immune to her Songs.

"Please," said Lyranel. "Don't give me away. I have to get to my father. Will you help me?"

Elsie shook her head. "More'n I'm worth to let you go, *Lady*."

"I'll... I'll give you all my jewels," said Lyranel.



"Jewels?" Elsie licked her lips, then frowned. "What jewels? Don't look like you have none on you right now."

"They're in my saddlebags," said Lyranel. "On... oh." Diamond had run off with them. "I promise, once I get to our castle, I'll give you lots of them."

Elsie sniffed. "Oh, sure. Like as not, you'll have me clapped in irons. Try something else."

"I don't have anything else," said Lyranel.

"Then I might as well go wake them all," said Elsie, turning away.

"Wait!" said Lyranel. "What do you want?"

"Teach me," said Elsie.

Lyranel blinked. "Teach you to do what?"

"To Sing, of course," said Elsie. "Properly, like. That would be a useful skill. Could put guards to sleep, so that we could get into granaries and stuff."

"Singing to steal? Oh, no. I couldn't teach you if you were going to do that. You mustn't use Songs for evil intent."

"Well, what good are they then? If I can't use them to help feed us?" asked Elsie. She flapped her hand at Lyranel. "Never mind, then. I'll go wake up Mhaire. The sooner we get you to those slavers, the better."



"No, wait, please!" said Lyranel. "Fine. If you help me escape, I'll teach you."

Elsie spat on her hand and held it out. "Done."

Lyranel blinked, then carefully spat on her own hand. Elsie grabbed it and shook once.

"All right, let's go," said Elsie. She took a few steps towards the woods, then turned and waited. "Are you coming, or not?"

"I... I can't," said Lyranel.

"Oh, right, the feet," said Elsie. "Cow plop. I forgot. Guess you'll have to lean on me."

She put her shoulder under Lyranel's arm and lifted her slightly. Step by painful step, they walked away from the sleeping bandits. Lyranel concentrated on putting one foot in front of the other, willing herself to keep silent as they moved deeper into the darkened woods.

"Wait!" she said, suddenly remembering. "What about Lord Evander?"

"Him?" said Elsie. "Never mind him. He'll be fine."



"But—"

"Listen, if we go back for him, it'll take longer. And Mhaire and the others might wake up. You don't want that, do you?"

"No, but..."

"Then let's go."

"What about your parents? Won't they miss you?"

"Enough questions, yer Ladyship. Don't you want to escape?"

Elsie led Lyranel further and further away, on a deer path that paralleled a tiny stream. Lyranel bit her lip at the pain in her ankles and feet. The path was strewn with branches and small rocks. Lyranel stubbed her toe on one and cried out.

"Ssh!" said Elsie. "You'll have them on us. And we don't move that fast, thanks to you, Mistress Useless."

"If only I had my crutches," Lyranel groaned. "I can go a lot faster with them."

"Crutches, eh?" asked Elsie. She let Lyranel drop to the ground. "Stay there. I'll be right back."



Elsie stepped into the underbrush and was gone.

"Elsie?" Lyranel called. There was no answer. She slumped over her aching feet, wishing that Nan was there to give them a rub.

"Lyranel," said a quiet voice. She couldn't tell if it was a man or a woman.

"Elsie?" asked Lyranel, peering into the dark, tangled woods. "Is that you?"

"Lyranel," the voice repeated.

"Who's there? Come out!"

"Lyranel."

Lyranel clapped her hands over her ears. "Warts!" When she lowered them again, there was silence. "Is anyone there?"

There was a rustling in the trees, and Lyranel shrank back. Then Elsie came striding into the open. "Here," she said, handing Lyranel two long *y*-shaped willow branches.

Lyranel took a deep breath, then took the crutches and inched her way upright. The makeshift crutches fit just under her armpits. She grinned. "They're perfect. How did you know my size?"



"Bandits get used to making good guesses," said Elsie, with a smirk.

"Thank you," said Lyranel. She took a step, then another, getting back into the rhythm. They weren't as comfortable as her hand-carved, padded crutches, but they worked just fine. "Well, what are you waiting for? Let's go."

She stabbed the ground with the crutches, then let her legs swing forward, practically flying down the path.

"Hey, wait for me," said Elsie. "Cow plop, but those really do make a difference!"

"Not so useless now, am I?" Lyranel yelled back.

"Quiet, you idiot," said Elsie, hurrying behind. "Nobles! Not a brain in their heads."

"Where are we going?" asked Lyranel.

"There's a woodsman's shack east of here. We'll head off north, then double back to the shack. We couldn't help but leave a trail even a blind man could read, but maybe we can mess the trackers up a little."



"I thought I heard a voice, back there," said Lyranel. "Someone called my name."

"A voice? Cow plop. They may be tracking us already. Let's hurry."

Elsie pushed past Lyranel, then stepped into the stream beside the path. "Yeep, that's cold. Come on. Our tracks will be harder to find this way." She snickered. "And I'll bet Hamish won't know what to make of your crutches." They followed the stream for a little while, then stepped out of it onto some rocks. "All right, now we circle back east."

"Are you sure you know where you're going?" asked Lyranel.

"Been livin' in the woods since I was a baby," said Elsie.

Lyranel followed Elsie, trusting to the bandit girl's knowledge. It was growing lighter, and her feet and ankles were starting to hurt again, when they finally stopped.

"There it is," said Elsie. She pointed to a small wooden building that they could just see through the trees.

"It doesn't look very sturdy," said Lyranel, eyeing the building's slanting boards and tilted roof.



"It'll do," said Elsie. "We can rest here for a while."

"Are we anywhere near the road to my home?"

Elsie snorted. "That's the first place Mhaire would look, silly. We're going to head cross-country till we find someone who'll take us there. More likely to be someone up and about later, than in the middle of the night. Now, come on." She tugged on Lyranel's arm, urging her towards the shack. The door was barred on the outside, and when they tried to open it, it appeared to be barred on the inside as well. Elsie picked up a stout stick and wiggled it through a crack in the boards, to lift the inner bar. It wasn't long before they were in.

The inside of the shack was in considerably better shape than the outside had looked. There was a slatted bed frame, a table and some strongly-built shelves, plus several chests which, when they looked into them, proved to be full of blankets, grain and other supplies. Flint rock and tinder lay inside a small box, along with an oil lamp. There was even a ceramic cask full of clean water. Elsie let out a low whistle as she let the inner bar drop back into place.



"This woodsman likes to be prepared," she said. "I wonder..." She struck sparks from the flint and lit the lamp, then looked closely at the floor, absently pocketing the stone. "Aha!"

"What is it?"

"I think I see a trapdoor. It's pretty well hidden." She dug her fingers under the wood, and lifted what had looked like part of the floor to Lyranel's unpracticed eyes. "There's a ladder. You coming?"

"With these?" Lyranel asked, lifting one of her crutches. "No, thank you."

"Fine," said Elsie. She clambered down the ladder. "Cow plop!" she said, her voice muffled.

"What's wrong?" asked Lyranel.

"Furs! Dozens of 'em. Whoever owns this is no woodsman. He must be a poacher. I found a bolthole tunnel that probably leads outdoors." Elsie climbed the ladder again, her head emerging above the shack's floor.

"Oh, this is awful," said Lyranel.

"Awful? Why? It's a great little place," said Elsie, as she let the trapdoor slam shut.



"No, no... bandits, poachers... my father will be very upset to know that this sort of thing is going on in his lands. He thought he had cleaned all the bandits out years ago."

"Naw. Can't catch all of us."

"My father talked about that. Actually, he was yelling. At the Captain of the Guard. One or two bandits had been captured, but the Captain said the rest always seemed to slip away, like mist."

"Huh. We know how to hide from soldiers. And there's lots of us. It's the Duke's own fault, y'know."

"What do you mean?"

"It's because of the Singing. Because there wasn't any allowed for ten years. Crops went bad, animals sickened, land wouldn't produce—what else can a person do except turn bandit, when he has nothing else? Or poach, for food and furs to sell?" said Elsie. "That's why Mhaire got us all together."

"Well, it shouldn't be happening," said Lyranel.

Elsie shrugged. "It ain't a bad life."

"That's not the point. And what about those whom you rob?" she asked. "And kidnap. To sell to the slavers." She was startled by Elsie's chuckle. "Now what?"



"Wasn't no slavers," said Elsie. "I was just yankin' on ya."

"There weren't? So it really was for the ransom. And Lord Evander will be safe."

"Why you worried about him? I told you, he'll be fine."

"No, he won't! Your chieftain will probably torture him to find out where I went."

"Not likely." Elsie snorted. "It was him who staged the ambush."

"Lord Evander? Don't be ridiculous. Why would he? And besides, he was with us the whole time."

"Ha. Your Lord Evander came to talk to Mhaire a couple o' weeks ago. You remember a wool merchant who rode along with you for a time the other day?" asked Elsie. Lyranel nodded. "He was one of ours. Marcus used to be a merchant; he could play the part. Lord high'n'mighty signaled him to set off the ambush later on. So we did."

"But why?"

"Who knows? But believe me, it was him. I recognized him."



"Then why would he play along as if he were captured, too?" asked Lyranel.

Elsie shrugged. "Some kind o' game, I guess. Maybe he wanted to impress you."

Lyranel sagged onto the bed frame. "It… doesn't make sense."

"Now—" Elsie began.

There was a banging on the shack's wall. Both girls looked up, startled.

"Lady Lyranel? Are you in there?" It was Lord Evander's voice.

# Chapter Seven

Elsie immediately clamped her hand over Lyranel's mouth. "Not a word," she whispered.

"Lyranel?" Lord Evander repeated. "Come on, I know you're in there." He rattled the door.

Lyranel tried to peel Elsie's fingers off her face. Elsie tugged her towards the wall, where she peeked out through a knothole in the wood.

"Huh," she said in a low voice. "That's him, all right. Come look." She eased Lyranel up to where she could look out the peephole as well.

Lord Evander was peering at the door, and pushing. "Lyranel! I said come out, child." As he spoke, he drew his sword and wiggled it into a crack below the locking bar, in much the same way as Elsie had used her stick.

Lyranel frowned and gently tugged at Elsie's hand, still over her mouth. The bandit girl reluctantly lowered it. "Didn't your people take his sword away from him?" Lyranel asked.

"Yes! And how would he get it back unless they let him have it?"

"He... he might have defeated them all, and escaped that way," said Lyranel.

"Last we saw, he was asleep, just like the rest of them," said Elsie

"He must have woken up first."

Elsie made a growling sound, deep in her throat. "What's it take to convince you?"

"Look, Lyranel," said Lord Evander. "I know you and your little friend are there. Won't you come out, please? You know I won't hurt you. I can wait."

Lyranel peeked out again. Lord Evander was still trying to work his sword into the crack below the locking bar.

"If he can wait for us to come out, why is he trying so hard to get in?" Lyranel murmured.

"Now do you believe me?" asked Elsie. Lyranel nodded. "Finally!" She pulled Lyranel to her feet and gave her a shove towards the trapdoor.

"I can't go down there!" Lyranel said.

"It's only a few steps," Elsie said, opening the door. "I thought you said you weren't useless." She disappeared into the hole.

Lyranel set her lips in a thin line. "Fine." She wriggled to the floor, then tossed her crutches down.

"Cow plop! You almost hit me," said Elsie.

"Sorry," Lyranel muttered. She slithered closer to the hole and lowered herself into it, reached a rung with one booted foot. She gripped the ladder with both hands and climbed down, letting her feet dangle. At last, she reached the bottom and collapsed on the dirt floor. Elsie clambered up again to shut the trapdoor and they were in darkness. Lyranel squeaked as something with too many legs ran over her hand.

"What?" asked Elsie.

"Some sort of insect. Ugh!" Lyranel felt around for her crutches.

"You're worried about a few bugs? Worry more about what your precious Lord Evander will do to us if he catches us. The bolthole's over here."

"I can't see," said Lyranel.

Elsie grabbed the front of her tunic, pulling her lower. She ducked just in time, feeling damp earth brush her forehead. They crawled on hands and knees as the tunnel angled towards the surface, Lyranel dragging her crutches. She hoped the tunnel wasn't long; her ankles were throbbing again. Something squirmed away from her hand as she put it down.

"I think I see something," said Elsie. "Light!" She shot forward. Lyranel could just see her foot. She scrambled forward, pushing her way out onto level ground. When she turned around to look where they had come from, she could barely see the tunnel's exit. They were in a thicket, a fair distance from the shack, just visible through the tangle of trees.



"That's a well-hidden hole," Elsie said with appreciation.

"What if Evander finds it, and comes after us?" asked Lyranel.

"You're right." Elsie looked around, then pointed to a large rock, as big as one of Cook's kitchen cauldrons. "There. We'll use that to block it."

It took both of them to roll the stone over to the exit. Just in time, too. Muffled curses rose from within the tunnel.

"Wait," said Elsie. She sprinted to the shack. Lyranel heard the outer bar slam down. "All right, let's go," she said when she returned. "I wedged a rock in between the bar and the door."

"Are you sure he can't get out?" asked Lyranel.

Elsie shrugged. "It ought to hold him until we can get away."



"Will he be all right, do you think?" Lyranel asked, looking towards the shack.

"He has food, water and light. Why do you care? He betrayed you." Elsie pushed branches out of her way to find a deer path. "Come on."

"He's the brother of a Duke, and a noble. He deserves respect," said Lyranel, limping behind Elsie.

Elsie snorted. "He's not acting like one. Do nobles have other people kidnapped?"

"Well, no," said Lyranel.

Elsie shrugged and kept going. Lyranel struggled to

keep up. What seemed like hours later, Elsie called a halt. She stood with her hands on her hips and stared around her, frowning in concentration. Lyranel was about to ask what was wrong when Elsie glared at her.

"Well? Are you going to say it?" she demanded.

"Say what?" asked Lyranel. She brushed a lock of her hair, which had come loose from her braid, out of her eyes.

"That we're lost!" Elsie yelled. A trio of birds took flight, startled out of their perch.

"Are-are we?" asked Lyranel.



Elsie covered her face with her hands, her shoulders shaking. Lyranel dared to put her arm around the bandit girl's waist for a quick hug. "We'll find our way," she said. "Don't be scared."

"I ain't scared of nothing."

"Well, maybe you're just tired. I know I am. Let's rest for a while," Lyranel suggested. She was hungry, too. She spotted something small and white at the base of a tree. "Oh, look, mushrooms. We can have a break and eat some of those."

"Are you crazy? Mushrooms are poisonous."

"Not this type," said Lyranel, levering the button-shaped fungus out of the ground with one of her crutches. "I'm surprised you bandits don't know that."

"Huh. A friend of Da's tried a mushroom once. We found him swinging from the trees, naked, raving about how the birdcalls were such pretty colors."

"Oh, that was because he ate the wrong kind. You should be very careful about mushrooms, but Paul… Paul taught me which ones were safe. These are fine." She was about to take a nibble, when Elsie knocked it out of her hand.



"I'm not waiting for you to keel over. I'd have to carry you, then," said Elsie.

"Well, what are we going to eat, then?"

Elsie looked up and grinned. "You'll see."

She climbed the tree that the birds had shot out of, then came slithering down the trunk with something clutched carefully in one hand. She opened it to show Lyranel. "Eggs!"

There were four of them, smaller than a chicken's eggs, gray and speckled. Elsie handed one to Lyranel and lifted another to her mouth.

"You're not going to eat them raw!" Lyranel protested.

"What, you think we should have a fire? No way."

Lyranel plopped down to the forest floor. "Warts. Why not? I'm tired and I'm cold and I'm hungry. And I'm not eating raw eggs."

"You nobles. Soft and stupid. Someone might see it and find us, you ninny. No fire." She looked at the eggs in her hand. "Although, I gotta admit, egg-on-a-stick is good."



"Egg-on-a-stick? How in the world do you do that?"

"Easy. Tap a tiny hole on each end of the egg, then slide a thin stick through it. It takes a while to cook, but it's great if you don't have a pan. You—" she broke off, listening to something. There was a rustling in the woods. "Run!"

Lyranel struggled to her feet and followed Elsie. Branches slapped at her as she pushed her way through the brush, expecting at any moment to feel someone's hand on her back. Her arms ached from the strain of having to move so fast for so long. Finally, she smacked into Elsie, who had stopped suddenly.

"What's the matter?" she asked, panting.

"End of the road," said Elsie. "Look."

They were at the crest of a cliff, staring down into a prosperous-looking valley. The way down was a straight drop. The steep cliff curved away north and south, tangled with trees and brush. If they were to move in either direction, they would be slowed to a crawl.



"I don't know where we are," said Elsie, with a sigh.

Lyranel looked down into the valley again. Fields of new wheat and grazing sheep filled the valley floor. There was a curl of smoke coming from the far side, from one of the chimneys atop a large stone manor.

Lyranel smiled. "I do."

# Chapter Eight

The descent into the valley wasn't easy, even though they'd found a beast track much like the one that Cate's sheep had made on the cliff behind the castle, on their way to and from their grazing. The path zigged and zagged. Elsie slipped several times, grabbing at wool-tufted brambles to keep herself from falling. Her face and hands were soon scratched.



Lyranel had an easier time of it, having done a similar thing so many times on her way to Cate's cave. She was out of practice, but the rhythm came back quickly, as she used her crutches like hiking staffs, carefully navigating the path. The sun was high overhead when they finally reached the bottom. Sweat plastered their hair to their heads.

Elsie looked back the way they had come, panting. "Cow plop. Wouldn't want to climb that again."

"Me, neither," said Lyranel, sagging between her crutches.

"So where are we? You said you knew."

"I think this is the manor house of Sir Thomas and his Lady, Joella. I was here before, a year and a half ago when Cate..." She swallowed. "When Cate Sang for their baby."

"She Sang for a baby? Like the way you Sang for us?"

Lyranel hobbled through the wheat field, Elsie following. "No, not quite. It was a naming ceremony. Cate Sang him health and long life and happiness, and helped him to find his place in the world."



"You can do all that with Singing, too?"

"Certainly. And there are death Songs and marriage Songs and seasonal Songs, too. We Sing at the solstices and equinoxes to help the world keep its harmony."

"The whats?"

"The turnings of the year," Lyranel explained. "The summer solstice is when the longer days begin to shorten and the winter solstice is when they start to lengthen again. The equinoxes are in the spring and fall, and they mark the times of planting and harvesting."

"Huh," said Elsie. "And here I thought Songs were just for fun."

"Oh, that, too," said Lyranel. "The way you were Singing, yes. But there's more than that. When I put the bandits to sleep, that was the third level of Singing. It wasn't a Song with words."

"I know," said Elsie. "I listened, but you were just making sounds. It was strange."

"With that type of Singing, you can alter the world a little."



"Why didn't I fall asleep too?"

"Singers are immune to each other. We know when the other Singer is Singing, but it doesn't affect us. Cate thinks… thought that was why my mother couldn't heal my feet."

"Hey! You two!" someone yelled. It was a black-haired boy a few years older than Lyranel, trotting towards them on horseback. His blue tunic was neat and clean, and he had a silver-pommeled knife in his belt. "What are you doing here? Don't you know what you're doing to Sir Thomas's crops?"

Lyranel looked down and then behind them, noting with dismay the wide swath of destruction they had caused. In their hurry, they had trampled the green stalks of the new wheat.

"Our apologies, my lord," said Lyranel. "We were unaware of the problem."

The boy raised an imperious eyebrow. "Fancy words from a little ragamuffin," he said. "Who are you?"

Lyranel drew herself up straight. "I'm Lady Lyranel, daughter to Duke Trioste."



The boy stared at her for a moment, then burst out laughing. "Oh, certainly. And I suppose this bedraggled wench is your lady-in-waiting?" He gestured at Elsie.

Elsie's hair had come loose from its braid and was flying in wisps around her head. Her scratches were overlaid with sweat and dirt, and there was a large rip in her skirt. Lyranel realized she must look similarly unkempt.

"I assure you I am telling the truth," said Lyranel, with as much dignity as she could muster. "I must see Sir Thomas immediately."

"Oh, you must, eh? I guess it will be good for a laugh," said the boy. He turned his horse and trotted back the way he had come. "Well? Aren't you coming?"

Lyranel and Elsie hurried to follow. He led them over to a dirt path between two of the fields and then to the manor.

"You two stay here," the boy commanded, as he dismounted and disappeared into the stone building. Lyranel sagged against her crutches. She was perfectly content to stay still for a few minutes.



"Lyranel?" asked a young woman. "Oh, it *is* you! Mikal said a girl calling herself by that name was at the door."

Lady Joella ran outside to clasp Lyranel's hands in both of her own. Lyranel laughed in relief. "Yes, it's me," she said.

Mikal, who had come to the door, rocked back on his heels, his mouth hanging open. "You mean she really is..."

"Yes, Mikal," said Lady Joella. "She really is. But what are you doing here, my dear?"

"I... we... Duke Candelo's brother..." Lyranel didn't know where to start. "I was kidnapped," she finally said.

Lady Joella gasped. "What? By whom?"

"By bandits," said Lyranel. She glanced at Elsie. "Sort of."

"Bandits? My goodness. Are you sure?" asked Lady Joella.

"Yes," said Lyranel, with another look at Elsie. "I'm sure. It's a long story. May we come in?"

"Oh, of course. How thoughtless of me. Come, you can tell me the whole of it later. I dare say you'd like to clean up first."



"A bath?" said Lyranel. Her nose wrinkled. Even she could tell that they smelled bad. "Yes, please."

Lady Joella turned her attention to Elsie. "And who's this?" she asked, her fine brows drawn down into a frown.

"Oh, this is Elsie. She's... my friend."

Elsie looked startled by this definition. Her mouth twisted sideways into a crooked smile.

"Well," said Lady Joella. "If she is a friend of yours, she is a friend of ours. Come in, both of you. Are you hungry?"

"Warts, yes," said Lyranel. The greasy stew was only a memory.

Lady Joella led them inside, past the staring Mikal. The manor was not as large as Castle Trioste of course, but it was well-appointed. Rich tapestries hung on the stone walls, there were fresh rushes underfoot and there was plenty of solid, well-stuffed furniture. Lyranel noticed that Elsie's gaze lingered on the many silver candlesticks and pewter plates.



"Don't even think about it," she whispered to the bandit girl. Elsie jerked her gaze away.

"Here we are," said Lady Joella, as they approached the end of a long corridor. Lyranel grinned. She hadn't had a chance to partake of the manor's baths last time she was here.

Sir Thomas had chosen to build his manor near a hot spring. Great copper pipes that tapped the spring meant the water in the great stone tubs, set directly into the tiled floor, was always invitingly hot. Lyranel breathed in the warm steam as Lady Joella opened the wooden door to the bathing room.

"Do you need any help?" asked Lady Joella, eyeing Lyranel's crude crutches.

Lyranel smiled at the woman. "No, I'll be fine. Really."

"Come to the dining room when you're ready then," she said. "You remember where it is? Good. And I'll have someone bring you clean clothes."



Lyranel let her filthy cloak fall to the floor, then sat on one of the wooden benches that lined the walls and stripped off her clothes, including her boots and underthings.

"You ain't getting me in there," said Elsie.

"Why not?" asked Lyranel, looking up. Elsie was staring at the tub, her arms crossed. "It's just a bath."

"Baths are dangerous," said Elsie.

Lyranel smirked. "Just like mushrooms?"

"You can catch all sorts of diseases in them, my Ma said."

"Maybe in some baths, like the public stews," said Lyranel. "But not in these." She used her crutches to hop to the closest tub, then slid into the water with a gasp. It was hotter than she had expected. "Ohhh," she groaned, sinking lower. There was a stone seat set all the way around inside the tub. She stretched out her legs, appreciating the heat on her sore limbs.

Elsie shook her head in disgust and walked around the outside edge of the bathing room, as far away from the tubs as she could get, inspecting the decorations. Lyranel chuckled. She undid her braid, letting her hair float out around her in long strands. Clumps of dirt and leaves washed out of it as she swished it in the water, then were sucked out through a drain set near the edge of the tub.



Elsie kneeled by the side of another tub and dipped one finger in it. "Here, this one's cold," she said. "I thought they was all hot."

"That one's for after you've soaked in this one," said Lyranel, leaning back against the edge. "Lady Joella says it helps to cleanse your skin if you go from one to the other. Do you ever bathe?"

"'Course I do. Once a year. In summer, when there's no chance of catching the ague."

"The what?"

"The ague. Fever and chills, an' spewing." Elsie grimaced. "That's how my Granda died, Ma says. She didn't want to take any chances with me."

"Oh. Well, it would help with the smell, you know."

"What smell?" asked Elsie.

Lyranel rolled her eyes. She didn't think Lady Joella would appreciate Elsie coming to a meal the way she was. But she could do something about that. She pointed to a clay bowl on top of one of the many cupboards in the room. "Hand me a bar of soap, please?"



"Soap? Where? Oh." Elsie reached into the bowl and brought out a rectangular yellow bar wrapped with a pretty blue ribbon, then sniffed it. "Smells nice. Not like the soap Ma makes."

"Lilac or basil, probably," said Lyranel. "Those are Lady Joella's favorites." She held out her hand.

As Elsie kneeled down to give it to her, Lyranel grabbed the bandit girl's arm and pulled. Elsie shrieked as she lost her balance, then tumbled fully clothed into the tub. Lyranel grinned as the wave from the girl's entry washed around her. Elsie's head popped out of the water. She gasped and floundered, thoroughly drenching herself, Lyranel and the space around the tub. One of her flailing arms smacked Lyranel's ear.

"Ow," said Lyranel, grabbing Elsie's hands. "Warts! Settle down. It's not deep enough to drown in. Though if you thrash around any more, I might."

"I'll catch my death!" Elsie wailed. She clambered out of the tub and sat on the tiles, her arms clutched around her knees.



"No, you won't," said Lyranel, wiping water out of her eyes. "Just think of it as having your summer bath early. Take off your clothes and get in."

Elsie shook her head and sat huddled on the floor. She watched Lyranel with a woebegone expression.

"Well, if you sit there much longer in wet clothes, you really will catch the, um, ague. You'll get chilled. Look. You're already shivering."

Elsie bit her lip.

"Are you scared?" asked Lyranel. "Of a bit of water? Elsie, the bandit girl, afraid of water. And here I thought you weren't scared of anything."

"Oh, all right," said Elsie, glaring at Lyranel. "Don't look."

Lyranel obediently closed her eyes while Elsie stripped off her sodden clothing. She opened them again when she felt a wave of water that told her the bandit girl was in the tub, and silently handed her the soap. Elsie took it gingerly, then began to scrub her arms and legs.



"Wash your hair, too," Lyranel suggested.

"I'm gettin' to it," said Elsie. Lyranel leaned her head back against the tub and closed her eyes again, listening to Elsie's industrious splashing sounds. When they stopped, Lyranel opened her eyes a slit. Elsie was also sunk low in the water, with her head propped against the side. She was smiling.

"It… feels good," she admitted in a low murmur.

# Chapter Nine

The bathing room door opened, and Lady Joella entered, with an armful of clothing. "I've brought you clean gowns." When she saw Elsie in the bath, she smiled. She picked up Lyranel's and Elsie's filthy clothing. "Come out when you're ready, girls. The mid-day meal will be waiting for you in my solar, " she said before leaving.

"Food?" said Elsie, surging out of the tub.

"Warts!" said Lyranel, as a wave of water washed over her. "Settle down. The food's not going anywhere."



But Elsie was already grabbing at the clean clothing. With a sigh, Lyranel pulled herself onto the tiled floor and reached for her crutches.

Still wet, Elsie struggled into underthings and then into a pink broadcloth gown. The color looked good against her fair skin, which, under the washed-off grime, proved to be lightly freckled. Lyranel carefully dried herself off, then picked up a gray wool gown from the chair where Lady Joella had left it and slipped it over her head. It was soft and comfortable, though the fabric felt rough against her water-wrinkled fingers.

Elsie had brushed and braided her hair into a long plait, then tied it off with the same bit of dirty leather lacing she had used before. "Ain't you going to tie up yours?" she asked.

"I've never done it by myself." Lyranel patted her own still-wet mound of hair. Perhaps Lady Joella's maid could do it for her.



"Nobles. Useless," Elsie said, but it was with more amusement than disgust. She looked around the room, then pounced on the piece of ribbon that had been tied around the bar of soap. "Turn around." She wielded the brush much more roughly than Nan would have. Then she braided Lyranel's hair quickly and neatly and wrapped the ribbon around the end.

"Thank you," said Lyranel. "Ready to go?"

"I ain't never eaten with a lady before," said Elsie, twining her fingers together so tightly that the knuckles were turning white.

"Sure you have." Lyranel grinned. "Me."

Elsie snorted in reply. "So where's this solar place?"

"On the top floor," said Lyranel, making her way down the corridor. She stopped in front of a wooden spiral staircase.

"Can you do stairs? On those things?" asked Elsie.

"Of course," said Lyranel. "Especially these. Nice wide steps."

"Well, I wondered. You couldn't do the ladder in that shack," said Elsie, walking beside Lyranel.



"That's different."

Lady Joella was waiting for them in the sunlit room. "Please come in."

Mikal was there too, lounging by the fireplace. Lady Joella gestured towards four chairs set around a table by one of the wide, open windows. The table was laden with cheese, several types of spicy-smelling meat slices, bread, and fruit.

Lyranel lowered herself into one of the chairs and Elsie plopped less gracefully into another. Mikal sauntered over to sit as well. Lyranel took a few pieces of each type of food. Mikal frowned at Elsie when the bandit girl grabbed a handful of fresh strawberries and then loaded her plate with meat. Lady Joella only smiled.

"There's plenty for all," she said. "I can send Henry for more if need be."

"Where is Sir Thomas?" Lyranel asked, after swallowing a bite of bread.

Lady Joella's nose wrinkled. "Out riding. He heard a rumor of that awful land plague, near the mountain pass."

"I hope he is careful. My father says the plague is deadly."



"It is," said Mikal. "My father sent some men to investigate a patch of it on our north border. Only half of them came back."

"Your father?" asked Lyranel.

"Duke Vierre."

"Oh! You're that Mikal," said Lyranel. "I'm sorry. I didn't know."

"Guess that makes us even, then," said Mikal, grinning around a mouthful of cheese.

"He's my cousin," said Lady Joella, smiling at him. "Come for a visit."

"All by yourself?" asked Lyranel.

Mikal shrugged. "Except for my man, yes. Father didn't want me to come, but I insisted."

"You mean you sneaked out when he wasn't about and galloped all the way here," said Lady Joella. "Don't worry, I sent a message to your parents as soon as you arrived."

Mikal grimaced. "My parents keep me wrapped in wool, as if I were a baby, incapable of doing anything for myself. They didn't want me out here, but I wanted to see the plague areas for myself."



"It's because of your sister, Mikal," Lady Joella said gently. "They're worried they might lose you, too."

"But I'm not like her. I'm fine. Why can't they see that?"

"What's wrong with your sister?" Elsie asked with her mouth full. Mikal gave her a disgusted glance.

"She is ill," said Lady Joella.

"She is mad," Mikal corrected. "About a year and a half ago, Sapphira started to hear voices. She says they never stop. Calling her, telling her to do things." He shivered. "She sounds just like my grandfather used to. Our parents have her confined, high in a stone tower with no windows. That's the only place she can't hear the voices, she says."

"How awful," said Lyranel.

"I don't hear any stupid voices," said Mikal, frowning as he flicked a piece of the soft white cheese around his plate. "So he doesn't need to keep me locked up, does he?"

Lady Joella cleared her throat. "Well. Lyranel, you were going to tell me about your adventure. Don't leave anything out. Start at the very beginning."



Lyranel sat back and took a breath. "The beginning? Do you remember when Cate and I came to little Thomas's naming ceremony?"

"Oh, yes. Cate Sang so beautifully."

"Do you remember that I didn't Sing?"

"Yes, but I assumed there was a reason for it."

"There was," said Lyranel. She told Lady Joella about her Singing, and her lack of control, and what she had almost done at the feast. Lady Joella gasped at that.

"You Sang fine at our hideout!" said Elsie.

Lyranel shook her head. "I still don't know how I did that."

"She's a bandit?" asked Mikal, frowning. "She should be clapped in irons."

Elsie folded her arms across her chest and glared at him. Lyranel looked from one to the other.

"Leave be, Mikal," said Lady Joella, putting a restraining hand on his arm. "Pray continue, Lyranel."

"Um, yes. Cate and I decided that I really needed to go to Gavanton, to see if some other Singers there could help me. We set out, all of us, several days ago. And then we were ambushed by bandits."

"All of you? But you and Elsie were alone when you came here," said Lady Joella.

Lyranel looked at the floor. "Lord Evander... Duke Candelo's brother... said they were all... killed."

"Oh, Lyranel!" said Lady Joella. "But that is terrible. You poor thing." She rose and reached out to Lyranel.

Lyranel looked up into Lady Joella's sympathetic face. Lyranel had held off weeping for so long. Now that she was fed and clean and didn't have to run anywhere in fear, the urge to cry was overwhelming. Unable to speak, she leaned against the older woman's chest and sobbed against her gown. Lady Joella rocked her and murmured soothing words. Elsie patted her shoulder awkwardly.

When she could finally stop, Lyranel dashed the tears from her cheeks and pulled away. Lady Joella offered her a cloth, and she blew her nose.

"Thank you. I'll be all right now," said Lyranel, her voice thick. Her nose was still clogged, too. "Oh, I've ruined your gown. I'm sorry."



Lady Joella laughed. "Remember, I have a baby. Believe me, I've had much worse on my clothing than tears." She made a face, then grinned.

Lyranel giggled, then blew her nose again. It had felt so good to cry.

"What happened after you were ambushed?" Mikal asked. He eyed Lyranel's crutches. "How did you get away from them?"

"Elsie helped me to escape," said Lyranel.

"Really? Amazing. Why would a dirty little bandit girl do a chivalric thing like that?" asked Mikal.

"She Sang," said Elsie, nettled. "It was... wonderful. I felt like I was... part of the whole world, when she Sang. It was a harmony I could feel in my bones."

"So you were jealous," said Mikal.

"I couldn't see what the others were seeing. But I knew it was good. I wanted her to teach me so I could do the same thing." She popped a piece of cheese into her mouth and chewed noisily.

"What makes you think you can be a Singer?" asked Mikal. "It's not easy. I watched my sister Sing, before she went mad."



"Your sister was a Singer too?" asked Elsie.

He sighed. "Sapphira doesn't Sing anymore."

"Ain't you a Singer, then?" asked Elsie.

"No, I am not. And I'm grateful for it. All that running about, and all the ceremonies and the lessons. No, thank you."

"Lessons?" asked Elsie.

"At the Singers' Hall in Gavanton, no doubt," said Lyranel. "That's where I was headed. You should go too."

"But you said you were going to teach me," said Elsie. "I don't want to go to no Singers' Hall."

Lyranel sighed. "I can tell you some things, but eventually you will have to go there, I think. Cate said… that a Singer without proper training can be dangerous."

Elsie scowled. "Nobles. You can't trust 'em."

Mikal frowned. "I take exception to that, little bandit girl."

Elsie's eyes glittered. "I take exception to you, snotty noble boy."



Mikal rose out of his seat and Joella put a hand on his chest, just as Lyranel grabbed Elsie's hand.

Fortunately for all of them, there was a knock at the solar door.

"Enter," Lady Joella called out.

The door opened to reveal a gray-haired man in homespun wool, half-hidden in the shadows.

"Yes, Henry?"

"Begging your pardon, miladies, milord," said Henry, bobbing his head at all of them. "There's a young fellow 'ere, claimin' to be a friend of the Lady Lyranel's."

Elsie and Lyranel exchanged glances. Lord Evander?

"All right, Henry, bring him in," said Lady Joella.

Henry withdrew, leaving the door open.

"Lady Joella," Lyranel began quickly. "I should tell you that Lord Evander—well, he seems to be—" She broke off as Henry re-entered, gesturing to someone behind him. A tall figure squeezed past him, nodded, then stepped into the sunlight.

It took Lyranel a stunned moment to realize who it was.



"Paul!" she yelled.

*End of Book Two*

# Book Three

# Song

# Chapter One

Lyranel scooped up her handmade crutches and met Paul halfway across the room. She threw her arms around him in a fierce hug.

"I thought you were dead," she said, tears starting once more.

"Me? Nah." Paul blushed as he gently lifted her arms away. He touched the side of his head and winced. "The bandits tried their best, but I have a thick skull. Cook's told me that enough times."



Lyranel laughed shakily. "But Lord Evander said..."

"Him! I don't doubt it." Paul frowned.

"What happened? I was knocked out..." said Lyranel.

"Well, I'm not exactly sure, but when I looked up, you were gone, and so was Lord Evander. Cate was busy and didn't notice you'd been taken until later." Paul grinned.

"It was the most amazing thing. She Sang and that bandit's axe swerved right around her."

"Cate? You mean she's alive, too?" Lyranel pressed her hands over her mouth.

"Yes, of course. We're all fine." Paul's face darkened. "Well, not completely. But I'm sure Nan must be all right by now."

"Nan was hurt?" asked Lyranel.

"No, not hurt… but Cate decided to take both her and Fergus on to Gavanton, since we were so close. She said they had better healers there. She sent Toby back to your father, to let him know what had happened."



"Toby's all right? Last I saw, he was fighting a bandit with an axe," said Lyranel.

"He turned the axe and was only stunned," said Paul. "As I was. Cate had to Sing to wake us both up."

"But… but… everyone is alive?"

"Yes. We escaped the bandits. They chased us, but we ran the horses as fast as they would go until we came out of the woods, then stopped. They didn't follow us. That's where we found your Diamond. But not you."

"No, I was with the bandits," said Lyranel, rubbing the still-present lump on her head. "I Sang and scared Diamond. She bucked me off and then someone grabbed me."

"He lied!" Elsie said suddenly.

"Pardon?" said Lyranel.

"That Lord Evander. He lied to us. He said you was all dead," said Elsie.

"That's what he told me, too," said Lyranel. "Well, he didn't exactly say it, but I assumed…"

"Come to think of it, he didn't *exactly* say that to Mhaire, either," said Elsie, crossing her arms over her chest. "He went away after we took you—like a sack o' potatoes, you were—and when he came back, he said he'd taken care of it. Mhaire wanted to send some more men, but he convinced her not to, somehow. An' that means Hamish and them lied too. They backed up Lord Evander's story."



"Who's this?" Paul asked Lyranel, frowning. "Is this girl one of the bandits?"

"And if I am?" said Elsie, glaring at him. "What're you going to do about it, *boy*?"

Paul advanced on her. "I'll tell you what I'll do about it, *girl*—"

"Paul, stop!" said Lyranel, tugging on his arm. "She helped me escape. I never would have made it here without her. She's my friend."

Paul's head swung from one girl to the other. "Your friend? Don't be silly. You don't need friends like her."

"Yes, I completely agree," said Lord Mikal. "You really should stay with people of your own class and rank."

"Who're you?" Paul asked. His gaze roved over Mikal's rich clothing. "Uh, my lord?"



"I'm Lord Mikal. My father is Duke Vierre. And you are?"

"Paul. I'm a… kitchen boy. I came along as cook."

"He's my friend, too," said Lyranel.

"Really?" Mikal smirked. "You do make the oddest friends, Lady Lyranel."

Lyranel rolled her eyes. "I make friends with whomever I want. You sound like my nurse, Nan." She frowned and turned to Paul. "Is she all right?"

"I don't know," said Paul. "She took ill. As soon as we were out of the forest, Cate noticed that Nan was as white as her cap and sweating. She couldn't breathe right, either."

"Hmph. Sounds like food poisoning," said Lord Mikal. He flicked a glance at Paul. "Probably something she ate."

"It was not!" Paul began hotly.

"It couldn't be," said Lyranel. "We all ate the same thing that morning. Even Lord Evander."

Paul shook his head. "It came on sudden-like. Nan couldn't even ride by herself. Cate had to take her on her own horse and hold onto her. Fergus was able to ride, though his arm was fair useless. I hope they made it to Gavanton."

"You didn't go with them?" asked Lady Joella.

"No. Well, I did for a little ways, to see them safe on the road. But then I told Cate I had to go look for Lyranel."

"That's Lady Lyranel to you, kitchen boy," said Lord Mikal. "You should remember her rank, even if she doesn't."

"Mikal, I think I shall send you from the room if your manners do not improve soon," said Lady Joella, a hint of steel in her quiet voice. "Pray continue, Paul."

"Um, well, I went back into the forest. The bandits left a trail, which Diamond and I followed all day and night. It took me a while to find you, but I did eventually." He grinned. "I heard your voice. I came to the bandits' hideout just as you were putting them all to sleep. Had to plug my ears and close my eyes or I would have slept too. But when I looked for you again, you were gone."



"That's when Elsie helped me," said Lyranel.

"I know. I was coming to look for you, but just when I was ready to go, I saw Lord Evander wake up. I almost called out, but one of the bandits rolled over in her sleep. And then he was gone too!"

"How in the world did he get out of his ropes?" asked Lyranel.

Elsie sniffed. "Like I tol' ya. He wasn't really bound. He just wanted it to look that way."

"I decided he must have gone after you, so I followed him. But I think he went the wrong way. You should have heard him cursing. I didn't know half the words he used," said Paul, in an admiring tone. "He was sure mad at you. That's when I realized he had been behind it all. I got back on your trail before he he did."

Lady Joella broke in. "Wait. Do you mean to say that Lord Evander was the one who had you kidnapped? Are you sure?"

Lyranel nodded. "I wasn't at first, but I am now."

"So that was you, blundering around in the bush behind us?" said Elsie.



"I was about to call out, but you took off, like wild hares. I didn't think you could go so fast, Lyranel. I followed, but Diamond jumped a log and I… fell off. Rolled into a hollow." He rubbed his head again. "Conked myself, too. I almost passed out again and had to rest. Just as well. Lord Evander nearly stepped on me on his way past. He saw Diamond, though. He called out to her, but she wouldn't come to him."

"Smart horse," Elsie muttered.

"Wait," said Lyranel. "You said you were about to call out to me. Didn't you?"

"I didn't have a chance to," said Paul.

"Then who . . ?" asked Lyranel, puzzled.

"Maybe one of the bandits," Lady Joella suggested. "Go on, Paul. What happened next?"

Paul shrugged. "Lord Evander whirled, like he'd heard something, and took off again."

"I'm so glad he didn't find you," said Lyranel. "He might have hurt you."

"Come now," said Mikal. "Lord Evander is a noble like yourself. Even though he isn't a knight, he's still bound by chivalric oaths."



"Then why did he have me kidnapped?" Lyranel demanded.

"I'm sure that someone must have misunderstood. A noble wouldn't kidnap another noble. And besides, *why* would he have call to do something like that?" asked Mikal.

"I don't know, but I believe Paul. And Elsie," said Lyranel. "They wouldn't lie to me."

Mikal let out a snort. "Peasants lie when it suits their best interests. And bandits—"

"Mikal," Lady Joella said. "I have warned you, cousin."

"Fine," said Mikal, standing. "I know when I'm not wanted." He stalked out of the solar and slammed the door behind him.

"Hope he gets squirrels in his breeches," Elsie muttered.

Lyranel tried not to laugh. Lady Joella's eyes were dancing too.

"Anyway," said Paul. "By the time I found that woodsman's shack, you two were long gone. Again."



"You didn't let Lord Evander out, did you?" asked Lyranel.

"No, not me. I wouldn't have."

"I suppose we should send someone to release him," said Lady Joella. "Perhaps I should send Mikal. Though if this Lord Evander is acting in such a manner, maybe an armed guard would be a better choice."

"Oh, there's no need to let him out," said Paul.

"My dear, even if he did betray you, we should still take care for his person," said Lady Joella.

"No, I mean, you don't need to," said Paul. "He's already gone."

## Chapter Two

◇◇◇◇◇◇◇◇◇◇◇◇◇◇◇◇◇◇◇◇◇◇◇◇◇◇◇◇◇◇◇◇◇◇◇◇◇◇◇◇◇◇◇◇◇◇◇◇◇◇

"What! I wedged that rock in the door good and tight," said Elsie. "And it took two of us to move that boulder over the end of the tunnel."

"Maybe he found another way," said Lyranel.

"Tunnel?" asked Paul.

"It was a smuggler's shack," said Elsie. "There was a trapdoor that led to a back exit."



"Really?" Paul asked. "I never looked."

"Then how do you know Lord Evander got out?" asked Elsie. "He could still be down in the tunnel."

"I know because I saw him. When I came to the cliff, he was there. He watched this valley for a long time, then swore and headed along the crest, going north."

"Probably running home to his brother," said Elsie.

"I waited until he was long gone, then peeked over the edge myself," said Paul. "I saw you meet with Lord Mikal. It took some time for me to find a way that Diamond and

I could both get down. Had to go south along the crest for a bit."

"I'm glad you came," said Lyranel, smiling.

"I'm just glad to see you're safe," said Paul. His cheeks flamed.

Lady Joella coughed delicately. "Well, it seems that all is much, much better than we thought. Paul, we've just had our mid-day meal, but I can send for more. Why don't you join us?"



"Oh, thanks, my lady, but I'm just a kitchen..." He glanced at Elsie, who was smirking at him. She grabbed the last strawberry and popped it in her mouth. Paul lifted his chin. "Thank you, Lady Joella. I would be honored."

He sat in the chair that Mikal had vacated, and helped himself to a bit of what was left with deft fingers. Lady Joella kept her expression bland, but there was a distinct twinkle in her eyes.

"This soft cheese is very good, Lady Joella," said Paul, sampling some of it. "It's as good as my master's back home. You must have a good cook here as well."

"Thank you. I make the cheese myself," said Lady Joella. "Or, at least I used to. Before little Thomas was born. I'm afraid I don't have much time for that sort of thing anymore."

"Don't you have a nurse for the baby?" asked Lyranel.

"I did, but unfortunately, her mother fell ill and she had to go home to look after her. I hope she may return, but in the meantime, I must spend most of my time as mother only." Lady Joella smiled tenderly. "I confess I do not mind."



"Wait till the terrible twos," said Elsie. "Then you'll mind, all right."

Lady Joella laughed. "Well, I admit there are times when I could use a break. Sir Thomas is good with his son, and sometimes I can get one of the maids to help, but Henry is—"

She broke off as the solar door opened again. Henry put a foot inside. He looked panicked. "The… the boy's awake, your ladyship. And fair bawlin' 'is 'ead orff."

"I'll be right there, Henry." Lady Joella smiled as Elsie chortled. "You can stay here. I'll be back, I promise.

Yes, yes, Henry. But he won't expire if I take a few moments, you know."

Lyranel thought she could hear a child's cry, somewhere below them, the sound coming in through the open window. After a minute or two, it stopped.

Paul swallowed a mighty bite of meat and bread. "We should ask Lady Joella to send a message to your father, to tell him you're safe."

Lyranel nodded. "I wonder if Toby has reached him yet." She shuddered. "I can't imagine what he'll do."



"Probably wipe out that nest of bandits to the last man, woman and child," said Paul, taking another bite.

"What?" said Elsie. "For a kidnapping?"

"You don't know her father," said Paul.

"Oh, no, he mustn't," said Lyranel. "They're good people, really."

Paul choked. "What? Lyranel, they ambushed you, tried to kill us, and I assume they were going to hold you for ransom."

"No, we weren't," said Elsie. "Lord Evander was paying us. That's the only reason Mhaire risked her fighters on the open road like that. We usually keep real quiet-like and only jump idiots who wander deep into the Firwood."

"Well, anyway, they need to be punished for what they did to you," said Paul.

"Paul, even if they're bandits, they're still Triostans." Lyranel glanced at Elsie. "Aren't you?"

"Well, yeah, most of us. Some are from Candelo, too. Most of the little ones were born in Trioste. I was too. Ma said I was born in a seacoast town. I don't remember it, though."



"In a town? Then you weren't always bandits?" asked Lyranel.

Elsie blew air out in a rude noise. "No. Da and Ma were servants to some Singer, but she had to 'let them go', when she left. Da tried getting another job, but he couldn't. They only turned bandit later, when we tried to live in the forest by ourselves. Mhaire's band took us in, on account of Da being good with horses. Like I said, it ain't a bad life."

"Except that you steal from people," said Paul.

"We never hurt anyone," said Elsie. "Just take what they don't need and send 'em on their way. And we raid, and live off the land. It's better'n breaking our backs working in some lord's fields, without hardly anything to show for it."

"Anyone who works for a Lord gets to keep half the year's harvest on his section of land for himself," Paul pointed out.

"Big deal," said Elsie. "It's still working for someone else."

"Well, you don't have to be a bandit anymore," said Lyranel. "You can go to the Singers' Hall and live there."



"Me? No. If you won't teach me—like you *promised*—I'll just go back to Mhaire."

"But you can learn so much more in Gavanton."

"Oh, and who's goin' to pay for that?" asked Elsie. "I ain't got no money."

"There's no fee," said Lyranel, surprised. "Didn't you know that? The four Dukes and Duchesses—they put up the funds to train Singers. It's in the Compact. Even when my father banned Singers, he still paid his share. And of course, when there's a ceremony, like a naming or a wedding, Singers get paid for that. Cate said it all goes into a communal fund which they can draw on when they need it."

"So everyone is treated equally there?" asked Paul, making himself another meat and cheese sandwich.

"Doubt if *you* would be, bein' a Duke's daughter and all," said Elsie.

"Father did send me a personal allowance," admitted Lyranel. "Nan has it."

"Cow plop," said Elsie. "And Hamish let the fat old sow get away."

"Don't call her that," said Lyranel, with a frown at her friend. "I do hope she's all right. Well, I'll see her in a few days."



"What? You're not thinking of continuing on!" said Paul.

"Well, yes. I still need to go to Gavanton," said Lyranel. "And so does Elsie."

"I think you should go back to the castle. You'd be safer there," said Paul. "We could maybe borrow horses from Sir Thomas and ask for an armed guard."

"Or perhaps I could accompany you myself," said a man. Lyranel looked towards the solar door. Sir Thomas stood there, smiling, seeming not in the least surprised to see them. He was wearing brown leather trousers, muddy boots and a white linen shirt. "Well met, Lyranel." He strode forward and kissed her upraised hand.

"And you, Sir Thomas," she said. "How was your ride?"

Sir Thomas held out his hand to Elsie, but she just stared at it, a puzzled expression on her face. The knight smoothly turned the gesture into a pat to Paul's shoulder. Paul struggled to swallow his food and rise, but Sir Thomas waved him down and threw himself into Lady Joella's vacated chair.



"My ride? Not too good, frankly. I found a patch of that blasted plague, not too large, thanks be. Or rather, the dogs found it. We roped it off. I hope it doesn't spread."

"Oh, dear!" said Lyranel.

"Not much more we can do for now." Sir Thomas reached for a plate and piled it high with food. "Joella's told me your story, Lyranel. Someday I'd like to hear you Sing your adventure," he said, grinning at her. "But right now, I think Paul's right. You should go back to Castle Trioste. The danger is far too great for you to go anywhere else."

The solar door opened again, and Lady Joella came in, a chubby, red-cheeked toddler curled up against one shoulder. Sir Thomas rose and drew another chair up to the table. Lady Joella sat in it, and dandled the fussy boy.

"He's teething," she said. "I've dabbed some peppermint oil on his gums, but he won't settle down. Oil of cloves would be more effective, but I haven't any."

"Here, let me, lady," said Elsie in a resigned voice. She held out her hands. "Ma says I'm good with the little 'uns."

Lady Joella blinked, then handed the toddler to the bandit girl. "All right." Elsie held him expertly, and began to croon. It was a lullaby—not quite a Song, Lyranel realized, but still powerful. Little Thomas slurped his thumb into his mouth and stared at her, silent.

Lady Joella grinned at Elsie. "Would you like a job?"

Elsie snorted. "Babies is all right. But I got better things to do."

"Like be a bandit?" asked Paul.

"Like go with me to Gavanton," Lyranel said firmly, folding her arms across her chest.

Both Paul and Sir Thomas opened their mouths to speak, but Lady Joella held up one hand. "We need not debate it now. I think that Lyranel and her friends should stay with us for a few days, and then we can all decide."

## Chapter Three

"*Another* bath?" said Lyranel, a week later. She had come into the bathing room after supper, only to find that Elsie was already there. It was the bandit girl's fourth bath in two days. After her first impromptu bath, she hadn't gone near the bathing room for some time, but now Lyranel found her there twice a day. "Aren't you afraid you'll catch that fever?"



Elsie shrugged, making the water ripple in little wavelets. "Ma'd have kittens. But I decided I like baths."

Lyranel grinned as she laid her crutches down on the tiles and slid into the hot water. The throbbing in her ankles immediately receded. "I wish we had these at home. Feels good to be clean, doesn't it?"

Elsie sniffed the bar of soap she was holding. "Sir Thomas told me I smelled nice."

"Oho!" said Lyranel. It was hard to tell in the steamy room and with faces red from heat, but Lyranel thought that Elsie blushed.

Lyranel closed her eyes and relaxed, breathing deeply of the moist air. It rose from the water and was vented out above the castle via Lady Joella's greenhouse, which was on the roof.

It was so dry in Castle Trioste. Perhaps she could convince her father to add something like this. It would be lovely to soak in at the end of the day. She would mention it to him—after she'd learned everything she could in Gavanton.

"After this, we should work on scales again," she said to Elsie.

"Ugh," said Elsie. "I'm bored with scales. When can I Sing?"

"You need a proper grounding first," said Lyranel primly. When they got to Gavanton, she wanted no one to be able to fault her for improper teaching. She frowned, wondering if she ought to be doing it at all. But Elsie had insisted. Actually, she was a pretty good student, all told. "And we need to work on your—"

"I know," said Elsie, with a sigh. "My breathing."

"It's the basis for everything," said Lyranel. "If you want to be a real Singer, you need to learn to breathe." She glanced at her friend. "When we get to Gavanton, you can learn Songs."

"Maybe I'll just stay here instead," said Elsie, inspecting the end of her long blonde braid. "Looking after little Thomas, like."

"I thought you said you had better things to do. You want to be a nurse now?" asked Lyranel, chuckling. "Like my Nan?"

"Seems easy enough," said Elsie. "Lady Joella said I had a knack."

Little Thomas had taken to toddling after Elsie wherever she went, which left Lady Joella free to work in her beloved stillroom, creating her soaps and salves. Lyranel herself had been happy to sit and read in Sir Thomas's extensive library or ride Diamond, or watch Sir Thomas give Paul riding lessons and teach him how to use simple weapons. He couldn't use a sword, of course—that weapon was reserved for knights and nobles—but the long knife he let Paul have was dangerous enough. They practiced for several hours a day. Years of turning spits and lifting heavy cauldrons had at least given him some muscular strength. The rest of his time was spent helping Lady Joella in her kitchen.

Lyranel didn't see Mikal often, which was fine with her. He was prone to making nasty comments about 'jumped-up kitchen boys' and 'filthy bandits' in her hearing. He made a big deal about sparring with Sir Thomas, using swords and a suit of Sir Thomas's cast-off half-armor. Lady Joella didn't say anything, but Lyranel thought she was getting tired of her cousin's attitude, as well.



The two girls soaked in silence for a while. Thanks to the hot spring, the water never cooled off. Lyranel thought about transferring to the cold pool, but the heat felt so good on her body. Her head didn't hurt any more either. Rest and certain of Joella's herbs had helped with that.

"Why don't we do the breathing exercises right here?" she said. Elsie didn't answer. "Come on, I know you heard me."

"Oh, all right," Elsie grumbled.

"Sit up straight then," said Lyranel, doing so herself.

"I know." Elsie settled herself on the bench, then slowly took in a breath through her nose. Lyranel watched to make sure the bandit girl used the muscle below her lungs to expand her chest, rather than lifting her shoulders, as most people tended to do.

"Good," she said. "Now let it go between your teeth. I'll count."

They did the exercise several times, with Lyranel counting silently to sixteen, then letting the rest of her air out. Elsie did the same.



"Now, here's a new exercise. Hum a note with your mouth shut. When you feel your teeth vibrating, open your mouth as wide as possible."

As Elsie sang the notes, Lyranel noted with pleasure how the bandit girl had improved even over such a short while. She could even hear the 'ring' in Elsie's voice on some notes, the clear vibration that Cate had always gone on about.

"That's great. All right, that'll do for now," said Lyranel. "When we get out, we can do some of the scales."

Elsie frowned.

"I know you don't like them, but..."

Elsie shook her head. "It's not that. I thought I saw someone trying to see in through the windows."

Lyranel turned around and squinted at the steamed glass of the long window behind her. Light from the setting sun poured through—until it was blocked by a shadow.

"I bet it's that Lord Mikal," Elsie muttered.

"What, has he been peeping at you?" asked Lyranel, whispering. For all he went on about chivalry! "That's *not* a knightly thing to do."



"I... I don't know if it's him. But whoever it is, I don't think he can see nothing," said Elsie. "Not through the fog on the windows."

Lyranel laughed. "Maybe it's old Henry."

"Yeah." Elsie bit her lip. "Yeah. I guess it could be. But all week, that Mikal has been following me, see? And then when he finds me, he teases me. Calls me names. Asks me if I know stuff and then says I'm an ignorant peasant."

"If you know stuff?"

"Oh, ancient history. What d'you call it? Gee-ah-gra-something."

"Geography? Like duchies and kingdoms?"

"Yeah. And he says I should bathe more often. So… I think it's him."

"Hm." Lyranel frowned. "You stay here."

She struggled out of the tub and picked up the crutches that Elsie had made for her. Paul had brought her old ones with him, but the new ones fit her better. She had taken the padding from the shorter ones and had Paul affix it to these.

She wrapped a long robe around herself, then, out of sight of the window, filled a wooden bucket with cold water from the other tub. Putting a finger to her lips, she padded around the room to the door that led out into the grounds.

Lyranel quietly made her way around the outside of the bathing room to the window where she thought she had seen a shadow. As her eyes adjusted to the failing light, she could see someone standing by the wall. It *was* Mikal. He was on tiptoes, trying to peer past the steam on the glass. So much for chivalry! Planting herself firmly, Lyranel swung the bucket back and let him have it. Water sluiced him from head to toe.

"AAAGH!" screamed Mikal. "Th-that's *cold*! What did you do that for?"

"Serves you right," said Lyranel. "Watching girls bathe. You should be ashamed of yourself."

He hugged his arms to his chest as he glared at her, dripping. Without another word, he squelched away, nose high in the air. Lyranel collapsed against the stone wall in a fit of giggles.

Then with a sigh, she wiped her eyes and straightened. She listened to hear if Mikal was still nearby, but except for the lowing of Sir Thomas's cows as they came home to their barn, the evening was fairly quiet. She could hear the buzzing of the bees in their hives, industriously making honey. Even they seemed subdued, probably settling down for the night. No sign of Mikal, though. She stood for a moment, drinking in the sweet air, fresh off the mountain above them.



"Lyranel," someone called. It seemed to be a woman's voice.

"Yes?" she answered. "Joella?"

"Lyranel." This time the voice was deeper.

"Who's there?" she asked. "Paul, is that you? Sir Thomas? Mikal?"

"Lyranel." Now it sounded like two voices, or more, blended together. It seemed to be far away, weak and sad. "Help me, Lyranel."

Lyranel took a step backwards. Help? Help who? "Who are you?"

There was no answer. Shaking her head, Lyranel walked back to the entrance to the bathing room. Mikal was there, still wet, his hand on the door.



"Mikal?" asked Lyranel, her eyes narrowing. Maybe she should have thrown the bucket at him, too.

He snatched his hand away from the door and grimaced. "My lady. I fear we got off on the wrong foot when we first met. I... wished to apologize. Lady Joella... I have been... I have not acted nobly towards you."

"Nor to my friends," said Lyranel.

His eyebrows rose. "Them? Why would I have to?"

"Because they are people. They may not be nobles, but they are still people," said Lyranel, irritated. She was cold and her legs were aching again. "I thank you for your apology. Now, would you please leave? Go around to the main entrance."

"I can't. I told Lady Joella I wanted to take a bath since I'm already wet. She told me to use this door, so I wouldn't muck up her clean floors. I have to wait out here until she informs that filthy bandit girl I'm coming in."

"Stop calling her that," said Lyranel.

"She laughed at me, you know."

"Who? Elsie?"

"No," said Mikal. "Lady Joella. I think I've had enough of this place. And you. And your peasant friends."

"Oh," said Lyranel. Not that she would be sorry to see him go. "Then why did you just ask me to help you?"

"I didn't," he said sullenly. "Why?"

"I heard someone. A man. Well, a woman at first. But then a man. And then there were several voices. It was... odd." She looked up to see all the blood drain from Mikal's face, leaving it stark white against his dark hair.

He swallowed. "You-you sound like my sister Sapphira," he said. Before Lyranel could say anything else, Mikal pelted away from her, running into the night.

# Chapter Four

Mikal was gone the next day, his man and their two horses with him. They had apparently left during the night. Lady Joella told Lyranel and the others when they all arrived in the dining room for breakfast.

"Good riddance," Paul said under his breath, when Lady Joella told them. Elsie nodded in agreement.

"I'm worried, Thomas," said Lady Joella, as she cuddled her son on her lap. "He's just a boy."



"But not a baby, Joella. He has probably just gone home again," said Sir Thomas, spooning up his cereal grains. Making a face, he added more honey. "I'm sure he'll be fine."

"What if he wanders into one of those plague sites?"

"I showed him the places I'd found, on a map. He knows how to avoid them."

"But, Thomas…"

"Joella. He's old enough to make his own decisions. Let him be."

"I wish he hadn't left without telling us. That's not like him," said Joella, kissing the top of little Thomas's head. "He left a note saying he had to go. But no reason why."

"I… think that it's my fault," said Lyranel.

"Yours? But he liked you," said Paul. "It was Elsie and me that he couldn't stand."

"I… it was something I said, last evening," said Lyranel. "He said I sounded like his sister."



"He thought you were crazy?" asked Elsie, pouring a generous amount of cream over her cereal.

Sir Thomas nearly choked on his breakfast.

"Maybe I am," said Lyranel. "I thought I heard someone calling me. But there was no one there."

"Probably just your imagination," said Lady Joella. She patted Lyranel's shoulder "We live in a valley, and sometimes echoes can play tricks on your mind."

"I guess so," said Lyranel. "When I told him that, Mikal looked at me like… like I was a monster."

"Poor Mikal," sighed Lady Joella. "He just hasn't been the same since his sister..."

"Went loony?" offered Elsie. She shrugged when Lyranel looked at her. "Hope you're not."

"Me too," said Lyranel.

"Joella, if it makes you feel better, I'll go after him," said Sir Thomas. "The main road is too far from here. He probably went through the forest, and will pass through the mountains near the ruins."

"Ruins?" asked Paul.



"That's where the old Invader Kings had their city," said Lyranel. "The ruins are at the center of the four duchies. The Dukes and Duchesses broke the castle and city down when they rebelled, so that no one could live there any more."

"Invader Kings? Who were they?" asked Elsie.

Paul snorted. "Don't you know anything? That's why we have the Compact. You must know what that is."

"Well, sure," said Elsie, shrugging. "Who doesn't? Mhaire talks about it all the time. Mikal did too." She turned to Lyranel. "He said your Da vi-violated it."

"My Da? You mean my father?" asked Lyranel.

"He said Duke Trioste. I'm thinking he meant your Da, all right. What does vi-whatsit mean?"

"It means to break," said Lady Joella. "Or to stain."

"How could he? What a horrible thing to say about my father!"

Lady Joella sighed. "Well actually, Lyranel, I'm afraid your father did break the Compact, when he banned Singers from all of Trioste."



"I don't understand," said Lyranel. She laid down her spoon and crossed her arms.

"The Compact was all about treating the people of the four duchies well. The Dukes and Duchesses signed it, knowing that it meant they had to take care of their people," said Sir Thomas, waving the knife that he was using to butter his bread in a broad circle. "After they saw the kind of destruction that the Invader Kings had wrought, they swore to protect, never harm."

"Oh! Like an oath of fealty," said Lyranel.

"Yes, exactly."

"So, when my father banned all Singers…"

"He was, in a way, violating the Compact. Because he denied Song to his people," said Sir Thomas.

"Cate said some Singers stayed—in hiding."

Sir Thomas smiled. "True. But whether Singers stayed or not, it was his decision and decree. We—all of his knights—tried to talk him out of it."

"Duke Vierre and Duchess Siella sent message after message, pleading with him. Even threatening him," added Lady Joella. "He remained obdurate."



"What's that mean?" asked Elsie.

"Stubborn," Sir Thomas supplied.

"Oh," said Elsie. She shrugged. "Well, stubborn can be good."

"I think it was all that nagging that kept him from taking it back," said Lady Joella. "Everyone was pushing at him all the time."

"Except Duke Candelo," Sir Thomas put in.

"Lord Evander's brother?" asked Paul.

"Yes. He supported your father's decision. He has always been vocal about the autonomy of the duchies. He said it was your father's decision, and no one else had the right to deny him. So did the director of the Singers' Hall. I always thought it was odd that the Singers did not object as strongly as they might have," said Sir Thomas. He took his son from his wife so that she could eat more easily. "They accepted it quite meekly and went away. Except for your Cate, of course."

"She set herself up as an ordinary shepherdess," Lyranel said for Elsie's benefit.



"I dare say we are all glad she did," said Lady Joella. "For if she hadn't, you might not have gotten the help you needed, when you needed it." She glanced out one of the windows. Sunlight poured in through the glass in golden streams. "Well, I suppose we ought to be about the day's work."

"Speaking of which," said Sir Thomas, rising, "if I'm to go after Mikal, I should do so. Paul, would you like to come with me?"

A big grin spread across Paul's face. "Sure!" He swiped at his face with his napkin and scrambled to get out of his chair.

"He's probably hours ahead of us, so I doubt if we'll find him, but we can try." Sir Thomas handed his son over to Elsie with a smile. After kissing Lady Joella, he left the room, Paul at his heels.

"I would like to make some more soap today. It's getting used up at an alarming rate," said Lady Joella, a twinkle in her eye. "Elsie, do you mind looking after Thomas for a few hours?"

Elsie had flipped Thomas over her lap and was tickling his bare tummy with her lips. He chortled. "Happy to, my lady."



"But I was going to show you some more Singing exercises today," said Lyranel.

Elsie groaned. "Boring."

"Why don't you girls go out for a walk?" suggested Lady Joella. "You can take Thomas and do the exercises while you wander. I know your voice calms him."

"That might be all right," said Lyranel.

"Do we have to do scales?" asked Elsie.

"Well, maybe we can do some other things too. Cate taught me some lullabies," Lyranel said as she picked up her crutches and rose. "But scales first."

They walked along behind the manor, near the forest, little Thomas toddling along between them. The sky was clear except for a few white puffs, high up near the top of the mountain that towered over the manor. More mountains marched away north and south. Lyranel stared north for a moment. The message that Lady Joella had sent with one of Sir Thomas's men to her father must have gotten there by now. Her father might even be on his way south already, to find her and take her home. He probably wouldn't let her go to Gavanton. Not after what had happened. She shook her head and sighed.

"What's the matter?" asked Elsie.

"Nothing. Everything," said Lyranel.

Elsie didn't say anything. Thomas gurgled at her and reached out his chubby arms. She scooped him up, then frowned as she patted his bottom. "Oh, he's wet. Can we stop? I brought a clean cloth."

"Fine," said Lyranel.

"Cow pl-, I mean, my goodness," said Elsie, peeking inside his diaper. "This's a messy one! I'm going to have to take him back to the nursery. Want to come? I could show you how to change him."

"No, thanks, I'll wait here," said Lyranel. She really had no desire to learn that particular skill. Not yet, anyway. Maybe when she was older. Babies were all right, but she didn't have Elsie's fondness for them. She found a convenient stump and sat on it. "You go ahead."

Elsie shrugged and took off with a swinging stride, much faster than the leisurely pace of earlier. She was gone in moments.



Lyranel listened to the quiet. Insects buzzed, going about their business. There was a rustling in the bush behind her, probably a small animal. Sir Thomas had said he hadn't ever found anything more ferocious than foxes in their woods, although he'd had to chase a mountain lion away once, further south. She was glad when he told her he hadn't killed the big cat, just taught it a lesson.

Besides, if any large animal came by, she could Sing it to sleep. Lyranel frowned. Maybe. Maybe she could. Except for showing Elsie the exercises, which weren't really Singing, she hadn't Sung since escaping the bandits. She hadn't dared. Diamond, when Lyranel had finally gone to her, had shied away at first, though later visits had been much better. Cate would have been able to help with that, she was sure.

Lyranel rested her forehead on her crutches. She missed Cate and Nan. They hadn't heard anything from Gavanton this past week. She hoped Nan was all right.

"Lyranel."



Lyranel looked up, but there was no one there. "Oh, not again," she wailed.

"Lyranel."

"There's no one there, it's just my imagination," Lyranel whispered.

"Lyranel." The voice switched from male to female and back again. "I exist, Lyranel. I need your help."

Lyranel stood and hurried towards the manor. One of her crutches fell into a hole, and she stumbled, then dropped to the ground.

"Lyranel, please." The voice was soft, but insistent.

Was she hearing it with her ears? It didn't seem to be coming from any particular direction. No matter which way she turned, it sounded like it was right beside her.

"Who are you? Why should I help you?" she asked, panicked.

"I am dying, Lyranel. I need you."

"Me? What can I do?"

"You can help me, dear Lyranel. I heard you. I heard you when you Sang."

"When I Sang? Are you one of the bandits?" asked Lyranel. Her breath was coming in short gasps.



"No..." The voice faded for a moment. Then it returned. "I am... I am... all. I am plants and animals and rocks and creeks. I am... home to many."

Lyranel found that she had turned so she was facing northeast. Towards Candelo.

"I am... the land," said the voice.

Lyranel leaped up and swung her crutches as fast as they would go.

## Chapter Five

Lyranel's hands trembled as she lifted the mug of hot chamomile tea to her mouth. She sipped, and the honey-laced liquid slid down her throat and into her fluttering stomach. Her teeth chattered against the clay rim.

"Better?" asked Lady Joella.

Lyranel nodded. "Am-am I going m-mad?" she asked.



Lady Joella and Elsie exchanged glances. When she had fled back to the manor, Lyranel had found Elsie and little Thomas preparing to go out again. Elsie took one look at Lyranel's white face, and took her straight to Lady Joella, who was in her stillroom, stirring a mixture of infused herbs. Lyranel had stammered out what had happened. Lady Joella had immediately put down her spoon and brewed the hot tea. Elsie, holding the baby, hadn't said a word all the while.

"No, of course you're not going mad," Lady Joella finally said. "I'm sure you're just reacting to what Mikal said. I'll have some things to say to him next time we meet, be sure of that. Now, drink up, dear. Chamomile is good for calming your nerves."

Lyranel gulped her tea. It did seem to be helping a bit. Her belly unclenched, and her hands had almost stopped shaking. "May-may I stay with you two for the rest of the day?"

"Why, of course, Lyranel. You just sit and relax. Or read. Or you could help me crush flower petals. Whichever you choose."



Lyranel nodded, happy just to be included. One thing she knew: she did not want to be alone. Not if she was hearing voices. She carefully put her empty mug on Lady Joella's worktable.

The three of them spent the rest of the day making soaps, salves and oils. Lyranel looked after Thomas, who had fallen asleep in a heap in the corner of the stillroom, while Lady Joella and Elsie went outside to pour the lye into a large cauldron, cloths masking their faces from the toxic fumes. When they had finished mixing the oils and lye and other ingredients together over a fire, they brought the cauldron back to the stillroom. Lyranel helped Lady Joella and Elsie pour the newly-made soap into oiled wooden forms.

"There," said Lady Joella, wiping her forehead. "That should make enough for me to sell at one or more fairs, at least. I will probably have to make more."

"You sell your soaps?" asked Lyranel.

"Yes, indeed. People come from all over to buy my soaps and lotions."

"They're wonderful," said Elsie, a smile on her face as she took a big sniff. "I think it might be time for my next bath, too."



Lyranel giggled.

Lady Joella dusted her hands on her apron and laid it on the worktable. "Well, it will have to wait until after supper, dear. We have that yet to make, and with Paul not here, you girls will have to help me."

"Can't we wait until he gets back?" asked Elsie. She licked her lips. "He's so much better at it than we would be."

"Yesterday, he said he was going to use one of Cook's special recipes for that duck you have hanging in the pantry," Lyranel added.

Lady Joella laughed. "Yes, I know. I've gotten used to his cooking too. Come on now, girls. We can do it. Besides, they might not return until after supper, and then where would we be?"

In fact, it wasn't until long after sunset that Sir Thomas and Paul arrived back at the manor, hungry and tired. They joined Lyranel and the others in the study, where Lady Joella was putting the last stitches into a new shirt for her son. She hugged her husband and sent Henry to see about getting two cold suppers sent to the room.



Sir Thomas dropped into his chair by the fireplace with a grunt. Paul immediately knelt to pull the knight's boots from his feet.

"Did you find Mikal?" asked Lady Joella.

"No," he said. "We found signs of his trek, though. He and his man must have been going in an awful hurry." He grinned at Lyranel. "You scared him, my dear."

"I scared myself," said Lyranel. She had been able to put off thinking about the voice that called itself Candelo, but it had been lurking there in the back of her mind all day. Had she truly heard the land itself? The idea seemed absurd. And yet…

"We did meet a messenger, though," Sir Thomas continued. "From your father, Lyranel."

"M-my father?" she stammered.

"Yes. He's coming. He'll be here in two days."

"To take me home?" asked Lyranel.



Sir Thomas shrugged. "Perhaps." There was a discreet tap on the door, and Henry entered bearing a tray piled with plates of meat and vegetables, and two steaming mugs of cider. "Ah, thank you, Henry."

Lyranel chewed on a fingernail, her emotions see-sawing. It would be good to see her father again, but not if he was here to bring her back to Castle Trioste. Gavanton, that was where she needed to be, to learn to Sing properly. And maybe the voices would stop, there. If her father took her back to the castle, he might never let her go again. Would she end up locked in a tower, like Sapphira? She gulped.

"Will you excuse me, please?" she asked, picking up her crutches.

Lady Joella gave her a kindly smile. "Certainly, my dear. I understand."

Lady Joella had been more than generous in letting them stay in the manor for so long. She would have to do something for her and Sir Thomas in thanks.

She had meant to go to her room, the one that she shared with Elsie. Somehow, she found herself outside instead, with no memory of how she had gotten there. She had been preoccupied with thinking about what she would do if her father insisted on her returning to the castle. Not only was he her father, he was her Duke. She had sworn an oath, promising to obey him in all things. In honor, if he ordered it so, she would have to.



She wandered towards the stable, where she found Diamond in her stall. The mare's ears pricked up at her entrance. She seemed to have finally forgiven Lyranel for the scare. No one had ridden the mare since the day before, and Diamond was frisky. She tossed her head and nosed Lyranel, inspecting her.

"I'm sorry, darling," Lyranel said to the horse.

Maybe she could saddle Diamond, and sneak away to Gavanton on her own, with no one the wiser until it was too late. She rested her head against Diamond's side. No, probably not. Her father would doubtless come after her.

The other horses, including the ones that Sir Thomas and Paul had ridden in their search for Mikal, were groomed and fed and mostly all asleep. The stable was quiet, except for the occasional horsey grumble.

"Lyranel."



It was the voice again. Male, this time. Lyranel sighed and closed her eyes.

"Lyranel."

"What do you want?" she whispered. No. She wasn't going crazy, and it wasn't her imagination. She knew it. Somehow, she knew it. The land itself was calling her.

"Help me."

"Help you, how?"

"Come to me."

"To Candelo? I can't."

"Please, Lyranel," said the voice, this time in that of a child's.

A wave of sorrow and love, longing and pain hit her. Lyranel sagged against her horse and would have fallen if she hadn't grabbed a handful of Diamond's long mane.

"Candelo?" she said.

There was no answer.

Lyranel staggered out of the stable and back into the manor. She passed the study, where all but Elsie were still sitting, and headed for her room, where she lay down on the bed and pulled the covers over her. She was shivering.



Elsie came in later, smelling of soap. Lyranel feigned sleep. Elsie crept around the room getting ready for bed, and soon Lyranel heard the rustle of sheets as the bandit girl slid into her own bed. When she could hear Elsie's faint snores, she quietly got up and left.

She told herself she was only going to visit with Diamond again. And of course, Diamond would appreciate a carrot or two. And if she was going to the stable, she might as well take a snack for herself. It wasn't until she had filched enough food from the kitchen for a long journey that she realized she had made up her mind. She ducked into the stillroom and hurriedly wrote a note for Lady Joella and Sir Thomas, telling them that they had been fine hosts, but that she had to go to Gavanton—even though that wasn't true. Instead of waiting for her father, she was going to travel to Candelo. That was the only way she would be able to get the voices to stop.

Outside, she made her way to the stables, helped along by illumination from the slim crescent moon. She saddled Diamond, then packed the food in one of the saddlebags, and slid her crutches into their leather thongs.



"Warts," she said, as she realized she hadn't brought an extra outfit or her cloak, both of which Lady Joella had loaned her. Should she chance going back to the manor for them? She turned around, and stumbled back against the mare.

Elsie and Paul stood in the entrance, their arms crossed over their chests. Both were cloaked and booted for riding.

"Looking for this?" Elsie asked, holding up a large bag.

# Chapter Six

◇◇◇◇◇◇◇◇◇◇◇◇◇◇◇◇◇◇◇◇◇◇◇◇◇◇◇◇◇◇◇◇◇◇◇◇◇◇◇◇◇◇◇◇◇◇◇◇

"You were asleep," Lyranel accused.

Elsie shrugged. "You learn to sleep light when you're a bandit."

"And I saw you go into the stable. You didn't really expect me let you go off alone again, did you?" asked Paul, grinning.

"I must warn you, I'm not going to Trioste. Or even Gavanton," said Lyranel. Paul looked about to argue, then raised his hands and shook his head.



"Fine by me," said Elsie. "I packed your cloak and things." She moved closer and stuffed the bag she held into Diamond's other saddlebag.

"I thought you were going to stay with Lady Joella," said Lyranel.

"Well, like I said, babies are all right. But I don't want to be nurse to one for the rest of my life. 'Drather go with you. It'd be a little more interesting, I bet."

"Aren't you worried that I'm going crazy?" Lyranel asked.

Paul shrugged. "If you say you hear the land, I believe you. Besides, I thought you were crazy when you set that fire in the castle midden when you were six. I guess I'm used to it."

"You set a fire?" asked Elsie, looking vastly impressed. "And here I thought you never did anything wrong."

"I just wanted to see if it would light," Lyranel said faintly. "With all those table scraps and broken crockery."



"And the distilled spirits that Cook had used to light one of his subtleties on fire the evening before," Paul added. "It singed my eyebrows off. I had a time explaining *that,* believe me. Look, Lyranel. Wherever you're going, you'll need me to cook for you."

"You need me to show you how to camp out," Elsie added.

"I've slept out before," Lyranel protested.

"Oh, you slept out. Right. In a silken tent, wrapped up in good wool, with a full belly and probably a sweet laid on your satin pillow. Believe me, this trip won't be like that," said Elsie. "Well, are we going to gab, or are we going to go?"

Lyranel stared at both of them, then nodded. "Thank you," she said, her throat thick.

They encountered no one else as they rode out of Sir Thomas's lands and headed south. They had decided to cross the border into Candelo through the mountain pass that marked the boundary where all four duchies touched, the same route that Mikal had presumably taken. Elsie and Paul took turns riding double on Diamond behind Lyranel. The mare was eager enough, but Lyranel didn't want to strain her by putting three people on her back. She offered to walk, but neither of her friends would let her. With two riding and one running alongside, their little party reached the ruins of old Kingston just as it was becoming light.



They stopped at the crest of the hill that led down to the ruins.

"Cow plop," said Elsie.

The ruins seemed to spread out for acres, dusty and gray. A few green things grew in the crumbling dirt. Piles of boulders and rubble marked the place where once a mighty castle and its city had stood proudly against the sky. Long pillars of carved stone lay on their sides, broken into thick disks that snaked along the ground. It was as if some giant child had tired of building with his blocks and had destroyed his creation instead.

"Can we go around it?" asked Elsie.

Lyranel looked north. The ruins extended for miles, right to the edge of the mountain range. "Faster to go through, I think."

"Does anyone still live here?" asked Paul.



Lyranel shook her head. "I don't think so. Alistair said the population was dispersed so that no one could claim the area as their own and start up a new kingdom. For the most part, the people were glad to go, since they had so many bad memories of the place. Although he also said it does tend to draw a… certain kind of person."

"What kind?" asked Elsie.

"Alistair wouldn't tell me. He did say this is the only place in the four duchies where Singing was used for destruction. According to him, it has a strange effect on people."

"Will it affect us?" asked Paul.

"Maybe not if we're quick..." suggested Lyranel.

Elsie leaned forward, squinting into the distance, her hand shading her eyes from the rising sun. "Thought I saw something moving down there," she said.

"Animals, maybe," said Paul. But he didn't sound sure. "Let's be careful, anyway."

"And let's go through as quickly as possible," said Lyranel. "I don't like the looks of this place."

"It's creepy," Elsie agreed, as they reluctantly descended.



Some of the stone walls still stood, towering over their heads. Someone had cleared a path through the ruins, so it wasn't difficult to pass between them, but they were still watchful. Diamond's ears flicked back and forth, the mare as wary as the rest of them. If she hadn't been feeling so nervous, Lyranel would have loved to stop and inspect the incised carvings on the walls and pillars. It was a kind of pictorial story, showing the beliefs and everyday lives of the Invader Kings. She turned away after peering too closely at one, however. Death and destruction seemed to be a common theme back then.

Something went '*plink*' behind them. They whirled to look, but there was no one there.

"Probably a rat," Paul said under his breath.

"Are you looking for a guide, then?" someone asked. Lyranel pulled Diamond up short.

The question had come from a man who seemed to have appeared out of nowhere. He was dressed in gray tunic and breeches, both items of clothing old and many-patched. A wide-brimmed gray hat was slung low over his eyes, shading his face. He was armed with a long knife like Paul's.



"A guide?" Lyranel repeated, swallowing.

The man leaned against a wall and waved his arm expansively. "I can show you all the best places, the most interesting, the most… chilling." His voice dropped lower on the last word. "Folks come from all over to see these ruins: scholars, students, Singers and thrill-seekers. I guide 'em through and keep 'em safe. For a price, of course."

"Thank you, but we're just passing through," said Lyranel. "We don't want a tour."

"Oh, well, that'll cost you too," said the man. Suddenly his knife was in one hand, and the other outstretched. "Think of it as a sort of toll."

"We… we didn't bring any money," said Lyranel. Her mouth was dry. She thought of lemons, as Cate had once taught her, and her mouth flooded with saliva. If need be, she could try to Sing them out of this danger.

"No money, eh? Well, how about that fine horse, then?"

"No!" said Paul. "I warn you, sir, I'm armed."



The man laughed and spit onto the dusty road. "Children. I can best you easily with this, boy. Now off you get, lass. I can sell fine horseflesh like that for a goodly sum."

"Guide, my foot. Why, you're nothing but a bandit," said Elsie.

"It's how I live," the man admitted with a shrug.

"Well, be off with you. Lyranel needs this horse. Can't you see?" Elsie pointed to Lyranel's crutches, attached to the saddle.

The man suddenly straightened, coming off the wall. He tilted his head up to peer at Lyranel's face, then more closely at her saddle, where her crutches were hung. "Lyranel, is it?" he said softly. "Hmm, yes. I never thought. . ."

He was interrupted by a trilling sound. He grimaced and disappeared behind the wall that he had been leaning on, instantly invisible against the gray stone. Elsie and Paul exchanged glances with Lyranel.

"Should we go on?" Paul whispered.



Lyranel was about to nod when the man reappeared with a woman in tow. Her long brown hair was tangled with leaves and bits of grass and her outfit, what was left of it, was in much the same shape as the man's. She hummed constantly, changing the pitch up and down the scale. The hairs on the back of Lyranel's neck rose. The woman was Singing.

The man shook her gently and she stopped, then resumed humming again, this time more quietly.

"I suppose introductions are in order," said the man. "This is Annice. She is—"

"A Singer," Lyranel finished for him.

"Oh, so you can tell. That's interesting. Very interesting indeed, Lady Lyranel."

"And who are you?" asked Elsie.

"Me? My name is... well. You can call me Rat." His teeth flashed in a grin. "That will do as well as any."

"How did you know that Lyranel was a lady?" asked Paul, frowning. He patted his long knife, as if to make sure it was still in its scabbard.

"Isn't it obvious?" asked Rat. "It's she who answers questions and gives the orders. She's dressed better than either of you two. She has a horse worthy of a noble." He sighed. "But I know because I have heard the name before. Many times."



"You have?" asked Lyranel.

"Well, certainly," said Paul. "I'm sure lots of people know that Lady Lyranel is Duke Trioste's daughter."

"Ah, but I heard the name from her mother's lips. She mentioned you often."

"You knew my mother?" asked Lyranel. Her heart pounded fiercely.

Rat gave her a sad smile. "To be sure. I'm the one who caused her death."

# Chapter Seven

"My mother died in a rockslide," said Lyranel.

"And I could have prevented her death. But I didn't," said Rat.

Lyranel shook her head. "Her death was an accident."

"No. It wasn't," said Rat.

"I don't understand," said Lyranel.



Rat took a deep breath. "Come," he said. "I have a... a nest, back here, where Annice and I live as best we can. You three look like you could use a good breakfast. I can tell you my story there."

"Why should we trust you?" asked Paul, his hand still on his scabbard. "You tried to rob us."

Rat shrugged. "Fine. Come, or not," he said, leading Annice away. He helped her over a broken bit of wall, with surprising gentleness. Annice followed him calmly. "It's up to you. If you're coming, it's this way."

Lyranel looked at Paul, who frowned. "He's probably going to kill us—or worse."

Elsie snorted. "What could be worse? Lyranel? Should we go?"

"I want to know what he meant," said Lyranel. "And… I trust him. I don't know why."

She shook Diamond's reins. The mare stepped carefully around the bits of rock, and Elsie and Paul followed. Behind the wall, the sunlight was abruptly cut off. They found themselves in dimness, with only the tops of standing stones still illuminated by the sun. Lyranel shivered. She could just see Annice's brown hair ahead of them. Rat blended in far too well to be seen, except as a moving shadow.



True to his word, Rat did indeed have a sort of 'nest'. His home had no roof, except a bit of stone that jutted out over a corner of the enclosure. It did have three walls, one of them with a hole in it that served as a window. He had arranged boulders around a firepit as furniture. Battered pots and pans, and other cooking implements were lined up on the ground. Rat was kneeling by the fire, poking at something that sizzled in a pan. Annice was sitting on one of the boulders, still humming and playing with her hair. She didn't seem to notice them when they arrived, although the clatter of Diamond's hooves echoed in the stone spaces.

"How do you like your bacon?" asked Rat.

"Honestly gotten," said Paul.

Rat chuckled. "There are wild pigs living in these ruins, among other animals. Rest assured that this fellow was hunted with no deception involved."

Lyranel dismounted from Diamond and tethered the mare to a handy protrusion on the rock wall. "How did you and Annice come to be living here?" she asked, sitting on a sun-warmed chunk of gray wall.



"Food first," said Rat, handing them each a spoon and a chipped plate on which he piled thick slices of crisp bacon, scrambled eggs and fried roots. He also filled two other plates, one for himself and one for Annice. He sat down beside her and guided her hand to the plate. She ate as if in a trance.

"Sorry about the quality of the dinnerware," said Rat. "Not what you're used to, I'm sure."

"Where did you get them?" asked Lyranel.

"The Invader Kings didn't take everything with them when they left," said Rat. "Found 'em down a dry well."

Paul sniffed at the food, but did not eat, watching Rat closely.

"Think I'm going to poison you?" Rat asked, popping a piece of bacon into his own mouth. He shrugged. "Suit yourself."

Lyranel picked up the dented spoon he had given her and ate some of the eggs. "It's good!" she said. "Thank you." She hadn't realized how hungry she was. Soon, her plate, like the others', was empty.



Elsie had been watching Rat eat and how he helped Annice to eat while she devoured her own breakfast. "I remember you now," she said suddenly. "You were part of our band for a while, weren't you?"

"Your band?" asked Rat.

"Mhaire's bandits," said Elsie.

"Ahhh, yes, the lovely Mhaire," said Rat, leaning back. He grinned. "A little too much woman for me, unfortunately. I had to leave."

"You mean she threw you out," said Elsie. "When you wouldn't rob one of the Duke's men."

"I couldn't do it," said Rat. He gently pried Annice's plate out of her fingers and set it on the ground. She immediately returned to her humming and playing with her hair. "You see, I knew him."

"You knew one of the Duke's soldiers?" asked Paul.

Rat sighed. "I used to *be* one of the Duke's soldiers. Unfortunately."



"Unfortunately?" Lyranel put down her plate and spoon. "You said you knew my mother."

"Indeed I did, to her sorrow. I was with her on the day she died. She was returning from doing a Singing for a peasants' midsummer festival. I was the one who usually accompanied her on her journeys, as a guard. She said she didn't need one, but your father felt otherwise. She said she appreciated having someone to talk to, at least."

Rat paused to wipe Annice's fingers with a cloth. With his face away from Lyranel, he continued. "I confess I was… a little bit in love with your mother. She was beautiful." He looked up suddenly. "As you will be. You look a lot like her."

Lyranel felt her face heat. "I've seen a portrait of her. A miniature. Father keeps it in his study."

"Yes, well. The journey had been long and tiring, and I was feeling a bit silly. We both were, I think. She commanded me to gather her a bouquet of the flowers we saw growing along the path. I remember them quite well. Bright yellow buttercups, they were. I and my horse trotted back to where we had seen them. It was then that the rocks came tumbling down. One clipped me on the forehead and my horse bolted, throwing me—away from the rocks."



Lyranel swallowed. "Why didn't she Sing them away?"

"She tried," said Rat. He closed his eyes briefly. "She tried. She was a powerful Singer. But she was so tired from the Singing she had done, and she hadn't had time to rest. She wanted to get back to the castle—and to you. When the dust cleared and I could see again, there was no sign of her or her horse. The rocks and dirt covered her completely. If I hadn't stopped to gather the flowers..."

"It wasn't your fault," said Lyranel. "It was an accident."

Rat shook his head. "When I looked up, I saw someone at the top of the cliff. I think he caused it. I tried to go after him, but by the time I climbed up there, he was long gone."

"Why didn't you go to my father?" asked Lyranel.

"Perhaps I should have," said Rat, "but at the time, I was too ashamed. I made up my mind that I wouldn't see him until I'd brought the fellow to justice. But… I ended up here. Haven't had the energy to move out of the place for years."



"Who was it?" asked Paul.

Rat frowned. "I don't know. A young man, about your age. I didn't recognize him." He poked at the fire with a stick. "Well, that is my story. What of yours, Lady Lyranel? Why are you here?"

"I… doubt if you would believe it."

"I've seen and done a lot in my life, Lady Lyranel. I don't understand some of it and never will. But there are very few things that amaze me, anymore. Try me."

Lyranel lifted her chin defiantly. "I came because the land called me."

Rat's eyebrows rose. "The land?"

"See? I told you that you wouldn't believe me."

"Oh, I believe you all right. I was just… well, not surprised, really. Just startled. I've heard that before, you see."

"From who?" Elsie demanded.

Rat nodded toward Annice. "From her."



"The land, the land," said Annice, in a warbling voice. It was the first time she had spoken. She Sang a bit, the notes a trill that echoed round and round the enclosure. Lyranel shivered.

"She heard the land, too?" asked Elsie, clearly appalled. She looked from Annice to Lyranel. "You gonna get like that?"

Lyranel gulped. "I hope not."

"She was like this when I found her," said Rat. "She had a companion, but he was dead. She was nearly dead, too. I fed her and kept her warm, but that's all I've been able to do."

"When did you find her?" asked Paul.

"Oh, three months ago, or so," said Rat. He eyed the sky. "It was still winter. I found her when I was in the north quadrant. She was curled up in a corner, still holding onto her friend. Him I buried, under some rubble. I think they came from out of Candelo."

"Candelo, Candelo," said Annice. "The land, the land."

"Can you help her?" asked Rat, leaning forward. "You're a Singer, aren't you? Can you Sing her back to health?"



"No," said Lyranel. "Singers are immune to each other. Perhaps in time, with rest…"

Annice abruptly stood and walked over to where Lyranel was sitting. "You. Are. A Singer," she said, very clearly. She stared at Lyranel intently, then her eyes glazed over again and she wandered away. Rat captured her and pressed on her shoulders to make her sit.

"She gets these spells," explained Rat. "It was during one that she said the land had called out to her, as well. I believed her, somehow."

Lyranel took a breath. "I'm still not sure I actually heard it. It might have been all in my head."

"What did it say?" asked Rat.

"It asked me to help it. To come, and to help. But I don't know what that means. What am I supposed to do?"

Annice rose and looked squarely at Lyranel. "Heal it," she said. Her knees wobbled. Rat caught her before she could fall and eased her to the ground. Her gaze turned to Lyranel. "Heal Candelo."

# Chapter Eight

"Heal?" Lyranel repeated. "What does she mean?"

Rat shook his head. "She's been saying that for days now."

Annice closed her eyes. "You have the power. I feel it in you. The land knows."

"What power?" asked Lyranel. "My Singing? But how can I help?"



"It is ill," said Annice in a thin voice. "Life has been taken from it. It sickens. It dies. Patches…"

"The land plague!" exclaimed Paul. "That's what she means. It's all over in Candelo."

"Land plague?" asked Rat, still holding Annice.

"Don't you know about it?" asked Elsie. "There's spots all over where you can't go. The land is dead, and anyone who goes there dies too. Haven't you noticed?"

Rat looked around the ruins. "Eh, well. I haven't left the ruins for years. Stuff's pretty dead here, most of the time. Don't know as I'd notice anything getting deader."

"Oh, you'd notice if you found a patch of the plague," said Elsie. "'Course you'd be dead then, so I guess maybe you wouldn't exactly care."

"Tell me about this plague," said Rat. "Annice has been talking about dying ever since I found her. I thought she meant her friend." He tenderly brushed the hair away from her face.

"I don't know much about it," said Lyranel. "Just what my father told me. It's patches of land where everything in them is sick. Even the soil. Animals shy away from them, at least the ones that can. If they are forced to stay there, they die too. Humans, as well."



"Dogs don't go near the patches, Sir Thomas told me," said Paul.

"Yes, they are able to warn the humans," Lyranel agreed. "They seem able to sense where the edges are and when one is about to strike."

"Are the patches like this?" asked Rat, smacking the dusty ground beside him with one hand.

Lyranel looked up at the stone pillars. "I haven't actually seen them, but I don't think so. This is old."

"Old, old," said Annice. "The land remembers. It ebbs, it falls. Many ghosts from Kingly whims. They went back to the land, all of them, in the end."

"What does she mean?" Elsie whispered. "Kingly whims?"

Lyranel frowned. "When the Invader Kings reigned here, they didn't treat their people well. A lot of their subjects died because the Kings didn't know how to conserve their resources. Or didn't care, which is worse. It took a long time for the land to recover."



"It hasn't recovered yet, some places in these ruins," said Rat. "Those old Kings must have been terrible folk."

"Kings' blood waters the stones," said Annice, still in that singsong voice.

"She's creepy," Elsie said under her breath to Lyranel.

Suddenly, Annice sat up and pointed at Lyranel. "You. Must heal. You have the power. Sing, child."

"I can't Sing," Lyranel protested. "I hurt things. I… make messes."

"Try," Annice commanded. "You must."

"But… it wouldn't do any good, here," said Lyranel. "There's no plague."

"You must, you must, you must," Annice said. "Please…"

"All… all right," said Lyranel.

Rat eased Annice out of his arms and stood. "We'll go find us one of those patches. North, deeper into Candelo. You said they were everywhere up there?"

"Yes, I think so." Lyranel shuddered. "But we could die if we don't sense one before we step into it."



"Won't it be obvious?" asked Elsie.

"Sir Thomas said they're not so easy to detect in the forest because of the denseness of the trees," said Paul. "You could walk right into one."

Lyranel put a hand to her mouth. How close had they come to dying, in their flight to Sir Thomas's manor?

"But it's all flat around here," said Elsie. "Nothing but grass. You can see for leagues."

"It's spring, though," said Rat. "It all looks brown and dead, until you get close enough to see the green shoots coming up."

"Then what can we do?" asked Lyranel.

"Easy enough to fix," said Rat. He put two fingers to his mouth and whistled, a high piercing sound that made Lyranel wince.

Elsie's eyebrows flew up. "Can you teach me to do that?"

An old brown dog with droopy jowls and floppy ears trotted into the enclosure, and lolloped over to Rat. The dog, a female, slobbered all over her master. He returned her caresses with rough affection, rubbing and patting her head, even kissing her on the nose. Lyranel smiled. No one who loved an animal this much could be all bad.



"Good girl, Dulce. That's my good old girl," said Rat. "We can take her with us. She can warn us."

"She's pregnant, you know," said Elsie. Lyranel looked more closely. The dog did have rounded sides.

"I know," said Rat, sighing. "More mouths to feed."

"Should we, um, take *her* with us?" asked Lyranel, glancing at Annice.

"I come," said Annice. She rose and started to hum again, then walked away. North.

"That answers that," said Rat. "Come on."

"Aren't you going to at least put out your fire?" asked Paul.

"And risk not being able to light it again? Besides, there's nothing it can burn," said Rat, following Annice. Dulce trotted at his heels.

"But—" said Paul.

"Come *on*," said Lyranel, as she stood. She grabbed Diamond's reins and used the chunk of rock she'd been sitting on as a mounting block. "We'll lose them if we don't go now."



Lyranel guided Diamond through the broken walls and rubble as Elsie and Paul scrambled to catch up. She could just see Annice's brown hair up ahead. There was something of a path through the ruins, though it zigged and zagged so much that Lyranel had no idea where they were. They finally emerged from the shattered city just as the sun was directly overhead.

Annice stood still, staring vacantly into Candelo. Nothing grew in the dusty soil in front of them. In the distance, tall grass waved, but no birds sang, nor insects chirped. They could see the skeletal remains of a tree, tipped drunkenly to one side. Just as Rat was about to step away from the dusty ground that marked the edge of the ruins, Dulce growled. Then she barked, ferociously. Whining, she pushed against her master's legs.

Rat squinted. "There's nothing there, old girl."

Lyranel clenched her teeth. She could feel it too, just like Dulce. There was a large patch of the plague right in front of them. It extended almost all the way east and west along the ruins.



"Stay away," she said. The others shuffled back into the shadow of the ruins.

Lyranel looked at the ground. Somehow, it seemed even more lifeless than the soil in the ruins behind them. Without thinking, she Sang, the pure notes spiraling up into the clear blue sky. She turned her attention downward, to the land, Singing to it as well. There was a faint echo of energy there. Not from the worms and insects who lived their lives in the eternal darkness of dirt, for they were long dead, but from the soil itself.

"Yes," Annice muttered.

But something was drawing that energy away from the land. She could almost hear it, a low bass throbbing, like a heartbeat. It seemed to come from somewhere up north—at least that was the direction towards which the echo bounced. Each throb smashed into the land and took more life away. Lyranel altered her Song to counter the sour bass notes. Her notes were louder and stronger. They wrapped around the lower ones and flung them away, back to their source. They did not return.

She turned her attention to the ground again. Now that there was no interference, she could sense that there was a spark of life, deeper down—tiny, but there. She Sang again, and this time she felt the spark grow, taking nourishment from her. Far below that spark, she sensed water. She called it up, to soak seeds left dormant, ones that still had a bit of life left to them. The grass would be stunted, but it would grow. She sagged against her crutches.

"Good," said Annice, when Lyranel had stopped Singing.

A wave of love and gratitude washed over her. Annice staggered, as if she too, had felt it.

"Candelo?" Lyranel whispered. There was no answer.

Dulce had stopped whining and was sniffing at the ground. She took one step forward and scraped with her paw. Her tail wagged.

"Looks like you did it," said Rat. "Dulce thinks so, too."

"How do you feel?" asked Paul.

"I'm fine," said Lyranel. "Why?"

"I remember how you were after you put that bear to sleep," said Paul.



Lyranel did feel a bit drained, but she didn't want to admit that the Singing had tired her. "Cate taught me how to conserve my strength."

"A bear?" asked Rat. "That's a story I'd like to hear."

"Some other time," said Lyranel, smiling at him in apology. "We should see if we can find some more of these." Her smile turned into a grin. It had worked! She hadn't hurt or destroyed anything. And she hadn't even had to control her Song either—it had worked just the way she'd wanted it to. "Let's go."

"Wait," said Rat. He ran back into the ruins and was gone for some time. Lyranel was about to send Paul to look for him when he reappeared with two mangy mules in tow. Their saddlebags were full. "These are all I have. We'll have to ride double, except for Lady Lyranel."

"You're amazing," said Elsie. "Where did you find them?"

"Here and there," said Rat, shrugging. "Told ya—the ruins are full of animals."



They worked their way northward into Candelo, with Lyranel riding Diamond, Rat and Annice on one mule and Elsie and Paul on the other. Dulce gave warning every time they came upon a patch of sickness. Sometimes she didn't even need to warn them; the plague's presence was all too evident, in the blackened earth and twisted trees, and occasionally a skeleton or two. No human bones, Lyranel was relieved to see.

She healed the patches as they wandered, countering the bass throbbing each time she did so. Elsie and Annice tried to Sing as well, but Elsie's voice wasn't strong enough, and Annice could not focus for more than a few minutes. Still, they did help a little. Each time, the land of Candelo sent Lyranel its gratitude although it no longer spoke in words. It seemed to be gaining in strength.

By nightfall, Lyranel had lost count of how many she had healed, small and large. She was bone weary, from more than just having ridden all night and again all day. Singing for Candelo was hard work.



A grateful peasant couple gave them supper of bread and meat and some truly delicious preserves after she healed several patches around their farmstead. They even offered the use of their barn for them to sleep in, which they accepted gratefully.

Hoarse from her Singing, Lyranel encouraged Elsie to Sing for the couple. She blushed when they complimented her. Later, they and Rat roared with laughter when Paul told the story of Cook and his bear. It was full dark when they finally retired. Up in the barn's loft, Lyranel found she couldn't sleep, for all that she'd been awake since the day before.

"I think I'm overtired," she said.

"Too bad I can't Sing you a lullaby, like you did the bear," said Elsie. Annice was already asleep in a boneless heap.

"I suppose we could try it m'Da's way," said Rat. "You get a bowl, see—a metal one. Put it over your head, and give it a tap with a hammer. The vibration knocks you out."

Lyranel winced. "That sounds dangerous. It would affect your brain to be battered after several, um, applications." Her own encounter with a rock had left her with a headache for days.



"Yeah, well, me 'n' my brothers were never what you'd call a bright bunch," said Rat. "Da said we'd best not depend on our brains, since we didn't have many between us. Besides, after the first taste of it, we kind of lost our enthusiasm for complaining."

"That vibration... that's kind of like what I think is killing the land in the plague patches," said Lyranel. "They are low notes—pulses that hammer the ground."

"Notes?" asked Elsie. "You mean like a Song? Could it be a Singer doing all this?"

Lyranel shook her head. "No Singer would do this. It's destructive. We work to improve life, not take it away."

"You said they did when they destroyed the Kings' city," said Elsie.

"That was different." Lyranel was about to argue further when a yawn overtook her. She wasn't sure when her yawning turned into a dreamless sleep.

They left again the next morning, after Paul had helped the woman cook breakfast. Lyranel was still weary, but she continued to heal patches of the land plague, calling up such water as was available from below to soak any dormant seeds that still held life. It was simpler to draw water up than to attempt to pull a rainstorm across the bright blue sky, which today was empty of clouds. Besides, it was getting easier. She could feel quite an affinity for the land, now.

"Good work," said Elsie, when Lyranel had Sung yet another ragged patch back to better health. She peered out over the largish area, inspecting it.

"Do you think you should rest? You look really tired," said Paul.

Lyranel nodded. "I don't know if I can do as much today," she said, sliding from Diamond's back. Paul caught and steadied her as she reached the ground. "Thanks."

"Are you hungry? Em and Yanni insisted we take some food," said Rat, taking some bundles out of his mule's saddlebag. "They—"

"Who's that?" Elsie asked suddenly. She was looking out over the healed patch, one hand shading her eyes. Lyranel turned to look. Someone was riding towards them in a hurry.



"Prob'ly another farmer," said Rat.

"No," said Elsie. "I don't think so."

The rider drew nearer, his galloping horse kicking dust and clods of dirt into the air. Lyranel thought she could see the glint of jewels on the horse's tack, shining in the sunlight. Not a peasant, then. They waited, watching. The man did not stop until he was right in front of Lyranel, yanking on his horse's reins. He kicked himself out of his saddle and dropped to the ground, then removed his wide-brimmed hat to reveal a snarling face, purple with anger.

It took Lyranel a moment to realize who it was. She'd never seen his handsome face like this, distorted by fear and hate. It was Lord Evander.

# Chapter Nine

"You!" Lord Evander yelled. "What are you doing here?"

"H-healing the land," said Lyranel, startled by the challenge in his voice. "By Singing."

His face twisted up into a sneer. "Oh you are, are you? I thought Singers weren't able to do anything for our poor blighted duchy."



Lyranel crossed her arms over her chest. "Well, I seem to be able to."

"You just rode through one of the sick patches, by the way," said Elsie, her pose much the same as Lyranel's. "You and your horse would be dead if Lyranel hadn't Sung the plague away."

Lord Evander glared at her, then glanced at the ground where he and his horse were standing. The horse, though blowing hard, with blood-flecked white froth around the bit in its mouth, was unharmed.

"What did you do to it?" he demanded.

Lyranel shrugged. "I just Sang, and brought up some water from below. The seeds that were still alive started to grow. There weren't many."

"Show me," Lord Evander said. "This is… interesting, but I need to see it for myself."

"We'll have to find another spot," said Lyranel.

"Shouldn't he be happier about this?" she heard Elsie ask in a low voice.

Paul helped Lyranel into Diamond's saddle once more, then climbed on his mule and pulled Elsie up behind him. Rat put Annice on their mule, but, like Lord Evander, opted to walk beside the animal instead of mounting. Rat kept glancing at Lord Evander, his brows drawn down in thought. Dulce trotted ahead of all of them. They'd only gone a short way before Dulce stopped abruptly, whining and barking.

"There's one," said Lyranel, nodding at the dog. "She knows."

Lord Evander frowned at Dulce. "So it would seem. Well, go ahead."

Lyranel dismounted, then straightened and Sang at the land. This was a small patch, but just as dead as the others. She closed her eyes, listening for the low throbbing that battered the earth. There it was—but it wasn't coming from the north this time. It was coming from somewhere to her right. She turned in that direction, then opened her eyes, to look into Lord Evander's. She gasped. *He* was the source of the life-draining sour bass notes.

"I don't understand," she whispered.

"No?" he asked, baring his teeth at her. "I think you do."



"You? The source of all this illness?" she asked. "But why? And how?"

"How? That's easy. I'm a Singer, too," said Lord Evander.

"You are? But... you can't be. Cate would have known if you were. She spent years at the Hall in Gavanton before coming to live in Trioste."

Lord Evander shook his head. "I never went there. No one knows I'm a Singer. Not even my brother. I do my Singing in private, you see."

"So you never had any training?" asked Elsie.

"Training? What for?" He snorted. "I taught myself. Nothing to it. I doubt that my brother would have let me go to the Singers' Hall anyway. He has always been 'training' me to act as his Castellan, to look after the castle accounts and tend the place in his absence. Never to be Duke, however. That is apparently not my destiny. My precious niece will be Duchess when her father dies, according to him."

"That makes sense," said Paul.

"Is that why you're not a knight?" asked Elsie. "Because you're this Castellan person?"



He laughed. "I'm not a knight because my brother is so tediously chivalric. He believes in treating everyone equally, even kitchen boys and bandit girls."

"So do I," Lyranel said, lifting her chin.

"Silly child. Who cares what happens to peasants?" asked Lord Evander. He lifted his lip at Elsie. "I don't know why I'm even talking to you."

"Your brother is a good man," said Lyranel. "What did he ever do to you?"

Lord Evander grunted. "After our father died and my brother became Duke, he graciously allowed me to be his squire. He said he would knight me. Then he claimed that I maltreated the servants I had on the land my father had granted me. No better than animals, they were. For that, he took away my ownership of the land and said he wouldn't knight me until I learned better. I was fourteen, and I vowed revenge. But shortly after that, the Singing came upon me. I immediately saw its potential for usefulness."

"For destruction, you mean," said Lyranel.



"Usefulness," said Lord Evander.

"Did you treat the peasants any better?" asked Elsie.

"Don't be ridiculous."

"So you never changed," said Lyranel. "And he wouldn't knight you."

"No. He bestowed the position of Castellan on me instead, as a sort of compensation, I suppose. I pretended I was happy with that, but then I decided if my brother couldn't see clearly enough to knight me, I would take what was rightfully mine instead. By Singing."

"You made the land sick because you hate your brother?" asked Lyranel. Her stomach felt queasy.

"I wasn't given what I deserved," Lord Evander insisted. "So I took it. I took the life, and the power. I Sang it into myself. It made me strong."

"It made you revolting," said Elsie.

"Elsie..." Lyranel whispered. "Don't..."

"The more I take, the stronger I become," Lord Evander continued. "And the stronger I become, the more I can take."



"Until it's all used up," said Lyranel. "Then what will you do?"

"Plenty of other lands around here." Lord Evander grinned. "Vierre was easy enough prey, especially in the early days of my experimentation. I haven't tried Siella yet. I couldn't touch Trioste, though. Until I got there. Something, maybe the mountains, prevented me. I found that out when I tried to stop that messenger of my brother's getting through to your father. I had to take care of him personally."

"Why would you care if a messenger got through?" asked Lyranel.

"Then, I wasn't sure if the Singers could stop me. Now I know," said Lord Evander, with a grim smile.

"Except that I can," said Lyranel.

"Hm, yes, that is annoying," said Lord Evander. "I shall have to do something about you. Originally, I thought you could help me work against my brother. I would have convinced you that it was in your best interest to do so."

"I like your brother," said Lyranel. "He's a little funny, but he's nice. I wouldn't hurt him."

"Is that why you had us kidnap Lyranel, then?" asked Elsie. "So you'd look good when you 'rescued' her?"



Lord Evander sneered. "Amazing. You figured it out. But thanks to Lyranel's Singing, which I admit, I didn't expect, and your clumsy help, she escaped first."

"You made fools out of my band," said Elsie.

"They were fools already, girl. They didn't need any help from me."

Elsie tensed, but Lyranel put a hand on her arm.

"But this is better," said Lord Evander, his voice light. "The people are already grumbling about my dear brother not being able to fix this plague. When I stop—and

I will, eventually—they'll want me to be Duke instead of him, because it will look like I saved them all. Now I can use you to heal these little spots, all the while taking credit for finding you, my little crippled heroine."

"I'll never help you!" Lyranel spat out.

"Oh, no?" Lord Evander threw back his head and Sang. It was a hideous, discordant sound, the notes off-pitch and so low that she almost couldn't hear them. Lyranel watched, horrified, as a patch of ground died, the grass withering outward in a growing circle. It reached the place where Rat was standing, and he cried out. His knees buckled and he swayed, then fell.



"Rat!" Lyranel gasped. He was doubled up in pain, his skin ashen, his arms tight around his body. Sweat dribbled off his face. Dulce tried to run to her master, but refused to put her paw over the edge of the devastation. She ran back and forth, whining. Lord Evander laughed.

"Shall I continue?" he asked.

"No!" said Lyranel. "No, please. Is he all right?"

Rat, unable to stand, crawled out of the circular patch of lifeless soil and grass, on his hands and knees. When he reached the edge, he reached for Dulce. She pulled him out onto the clean, growing things, where he collapsed, gasping for breath. Lyranel was glad to see that a little color crept back into his cheeks once he was free of the devastated area.

Lord Evander shrugged. "In time, I suppose he will be. I didn't take all of his life force. I could have."

"Is this what you did to Nan?" asked Paul, clenching his fists.

"I had to. She saw me take you into the forest," said Lord Evander. "Silly old woman. She reminded me of my mother, always telling me to listen to my older brother, because *he's* the Duke. I got tired of her prattling."



Annice came to stand beside Lyranel. "I know you," she said to Lord Evander. "You kept me. In a hole."

Lord Evander peered at Annice. His eyebrows rose. "Ah," he said. "It is you. One of the Singers that I intercepted before they reached my brother. I wondered where you had gotten to."

Lyranel glanced at Annice. "Did you do this to her?"

"No, she did it to herself. Listening to the land. Or so she said. She is obviously mad. Land is just land. It can't speak."

"You mean you can't hear it?" asked Lyranel. Not like her, or Annice, apparently—and perhaps Sapphira, Mikal's sister.

Lord Evander laughed. "You, too? Oh, how amusing. Trioste will be so upset."

"We came. To help," said Annice.

"And they tried, too. Which is why I had to imprison them. I put them both in an oubliette—a hole in the ground beneath my hunting lodge. They escaped, though, nearly a year later. I see she found her way here. I don't know what happened to the other fellow."

"He died," said Lyranel.

"No loss," said Lord Evander.

"The land does not like you," said Annice.

"The land! If you insist. Well, it will have to learn," he retorted. "Now, are you going to help me, or not? Or shall I Sing again? Perhaps for your little friends this time."

Lyranel looked at Paul and Elsie, then glanced at Rat. He was sitting up, draped over Dulce's back.

"Lyranel, you mustn't," said Paul.

"I know you now," Rat said in a tired voice. "You... were the boy who caused the rockslide. The one that killed Lady Miriana."

"It wasn't my fault," said Lord Evander. "She was just in the wrong place at the wrong time when I cracked the mountain face."

"Did you check to see if anyone was there?" asked Paul.

"I saw you," said Rat. "You were smiling, after."

"I was only pleased my experiment had worked." Lord Evander shrugged.

"I... don't believe you," said Rat.

"You killed my mother?" Lyranel asked. She gripped her crutches tightly.

"Yes, Lyranel. And I can kill your friends, too. All right, my girl. What's it going to be? Are you going to assist me, or do I Sing them to death?"

Lyranel hesitated. "I could fight you."

"What would you do? We are immune to each other's Songs, remember? Will you cause the grass to grow up suddenly and strangle me? Or the insects to bite me? Or perhaps this mangy old dog? Well, perhaps you could, but not before I killed her." Lord Evander crossed his arms. "Besides, what if you lose control? You could end up killing your friends by accident."

"I didn't hurt the bandits," said Lyranel. "I only put them to sleep. Which was what I meant to do. And I healed the land, too."



"Do you know how you did it? Can you count on being able to control your Song?"

"Yes, she can!" said Elsie. She looked at Lyranel. "Can't you?"

Lyranel hung her head. "I don't know."

Lord Evander took a step closer to her. "Come now, Lyranel. You are weary from all of your hard work, aren't you? While I am fresh and full of energy. Even if you could do something, what makes you think you could prevail against me?"

Lyranel looked at Elsie and Annice and Rat, who trembled as he hung tightly to Dulce, then at Paul. Paul shook his head at her, his eyes wide. She didn't know what he meant to tell her with that.

"Come to your senses, child," said Lord Evander, putting his hands on his hips. "Don't your friends mean anything to you?"

"Yes," said Lyranel. "Yes, they do." Her head came up. "So does everyone else, and the land, and the life within and around all things. You may not be able to understand that, but I do. I won't join you. Ever. Even if it means that we all must die."



She looked at her friends again. They were all smiling at her.

"Very well," said Lord Evander. He took a deep breath and Sang. As he Sang, a circle of destruction widened, heading towards the small huddled group of Lyranel's friends. Elsie and Paul struggled to pull Annice, Rat and Dulce away.

Lyranel Sang as well. Her pure clear notes clanged against his sour throbbing ones. As he tried to take the life away, she renewed it. The circle of destruction grew no larger. But how long could she keep her Song going? She couldn't just keep stopping his Song. She had to defeat him. But how?

Lord Evander's eyes narrowed. He turned to look at Lyranel and his lips curved up into a smile. He stopped Singing.

"What's the point, Lyranel?" he asked. "I'm stronger than you are. You can't win."

"I have to try," Lyranel said in a hoarse voice. Tears streaming down her face, she Sang again, as did he. His loud, discordant Song beat down on hers, smothering it.



Lyranel stopped Singing, her sides heaving.

"You see?" said Lord Evander.

Paul leaped forward, brandishing his knife. "Sing, Lyranel!" he yelled.

Lord Evander calmly turned to Paul and Sang at him. As the jangling notes washed over Paul, he jerked backwards, his back arching. The knife flew from his nerveless hand. He pitched to the ground, landing hard, and did not move.

"Paul!" Lyranel choked off.

Lord Evander turned back to her, his eyes glinting. He Sang again, the off-key bass notes pounding against her and the land around her.

"Lyranel," came a quiet voice in her mind. The voice of Candelo, the land. "Help."

Help? Help the land? But she couldn't... oh. Not *help the land*. The land *help her*! And Lord Evander himself had inadvertently given her a clue as to how.

Lyranel faced him and sucked in air until her lungs ached.



She called to the land, to Candelo. "Wake!" she Sang to it. The soil rippled. Green shoots burst forth in the deadened areas all around them.

"Is that the best you can do?" sneered Lord Evander.

Lyranel didn't bother to reply. She Sang with a strength she didn't know she had possessed, Singing to the land once more. She Sang of her friends and of her mother. Of her father and the love she knew he had for her. Of Cate and her teaching. And of Duke Candelo, whom she knew loved his people and his land. She urged Candelo to throw off its illness. To live. The land responded, healing itself.

Then she called to its fear and hurt, telling it who had made it sick. She felt its anger, from a spark deep down in the bedrock, far below the deadened soil, and urged that spark to the surface. Was it enough? Her Song was wavering. Then she heard Elsie's Song and Annice's warbling voice join hers, both of them trying to match Lyranel's pitch. For a few moments, they succeeded, adding power to Lyranel's Song. With all of the force of her being, Lyranel let go her Song, not knowing nor caring what the consequences might be.



Beneath Lord Evander's feet, the land lurched, then cracked open in a deep crevasse. He teetered on the edge, windmilling his arms, then regained his balance. He raised an eyebrow at her, then smiled and opened his mouth. But before he could Sing again, a form hurtled past Lyranel, and hit Lord Evander with a grunt, knocking the breath out of the rogue Singer. It was Rat. The old soldier's gaze locked on Lyranel's as both men toppled over the edge into the crevasse. The earth slammed shut, abruptly cutting off Lord Evander's shriek of fear.

He was gone, Rat with him. The land had its revenge on its tormentor.

Lyranel sagged against her crutches, letting her Song fade away.

"Rat," she whispered, her eyes wide. She trembled.

Dulce trotted forward, sniffing at the place where the crack had opened, then looked at Lyranel and whined.

"I'm sorry, Dulce," said Lyranel.

She slowly made her way back to Elsie, and Paul's motionless body. The bandit girl was Singing, Paul's head cradled in her lap.



"It won't do any good," said Lyranel, wiping the tears from her face. "We can't bring back the dead."

Elsie stopped Singing. "You did," she said. "You brought back dead land."

"That land wasn't completely dead," said Lyranel. "There was still a little life in it."

"There's a little left in me, too," said Paul. His eyelids fluttered open. "Thanks, Elsie."

"Paul," Lyranel gasped. She collapsed to the ground and reached out a trembling hand. "You're… alive?"

"I think so," he said. "Though Cook will probably kill me when we get back home."

"Why?"

"I forgot to get Em's recipe for those preserves," he said, smiling weakly.

"Oh, Paul," said Lyranel. She sniffed again, then laughed.

Annice came to sit beside them. Her eyes looked clear. "It's done."



Lyranel nodded. Candelo's voice was no longer in her mind. She could only detect a low murmur of continuous, healthy life around her. The land was content.

"You're Lyranel, aren't you?" asked Annice.

"Yes. Are… are you feeling better?"

One side of Annice's mouth twisted up. "It's like I was in a dream. But yes, I think I am better. Adam won't be, though, will he?"

"Adam? Is that the name of the other Singer who was with you?" asked Lyranel.

"No. That was Rat's real name. He told me everything; his name, his history. He talked to me… all the time. But it was like I heard it from a very great distance."

"Poor Rat," said Lyranel. "That was so brave. He sacrificed himself."

Annice nodded. "For you, and for your mother. Well, it is over now."

"Yes. I think the rest of the patches may heal on their own, without Evander constantly pulling their life from them."



"I suppose we ought to go back," said Elsie.

"Yes," said Lyranel. Would her father be there yet?

Elsie and Annice elected to gather the mules and horses, which had scattered. Happily, they hadn't gone far. They found all but Evander's horse. Elsie helped Paul to climb up on one of the mules and mounted behind him. Annice took Dulce with her, though the dog did not want to leave. They slowly made their way back towards Trioste.

A day and an eternity later, they were back at Sir Thomas's manor. They were met at the gate by a frowning

Lady Joella, who took one look at them and closed her mouth on whatever she had been going to say.

"Explanations can wait," she said as she bundled them all into the house. "Thomas went after you, but he thought you had gone to Gavanton. But never mind that now."

Hours later, after they had rested and soaked and been fed, they went to the solar and told their story to an increasingly distraught Lady Joella.

"Do you know if my father is coming soon?" asked Lyranel. Suddenly, she had a desperate urge to see him. "I have to tell him what happened."



"No need," said a deep, quiet voice. Duke Trioste strode into the room. "I heard it all."

Lyranel swallowed and stood. Wordless, her father walked towards her. He reached out his hand and clasped one of hers. Then he pulled her into his arms.

"Can we go home now, Father?" asked Lyranel.

"Whatever you wish, Lyranel," he said.

# Chapter Ten

Lyranel leaned out of her window and took a deep breath of the summer air, sweet with the smell of honey and green apples. She waved at Paul, who was busy digging up some early roots in the courtyard garden.

Cate shifted Lyranel's new crutches, ones that had been specially made to fit her new height, out of the way and sat beside her on the bench. Eyeing the crutches, Lyranel laughed.

"What's so funny?" asked Cate.

Lyranel smiled at her teacher. "It's just that, for someone who can't walk well, I sure did a lot of traveling," she said.

"Yes, you certainly did," Cate agreed. "Quite the journey, you had. They're already Singing of your adventure at the Hall, you know. It's a favorite."

Lyranel groaned. "Oh, no."

"People need stories like that, my dear one. Stories brighten a fire, and inflame the spirit. Especially stories of courageous maidens and valiant warriors, and villains who get their just desserts. They want to know that heroes exist and they want to believe that they, too, can have exotic and thrilling adventures."

Lyranel made a rude noise. "Thrilling, ha. I was scared out of my wits most of the time."

"Yet you still did what you had to do. That's courage, Lyranel. You proved that you are a Singer and most importantly, that you can control your power—when you really need to."



Lyranel nodded. Every time she had needed to Sing, she'd been able to. In the bandits' camp, for example, and when she'd been healing the sick patches. "I didn't control my Song when Lord Evander… died."

"You chose not to, Lyranel," said Cate. "It was up to you."

"What about when I was Singing for Duke Candelo that night, though? I couldn't then."

"Ah, but that wasn't really a dangerous situation. Though it might have become one, I admit," said Cate. "I think Lord Evander took advantage of it, though."

"And had me kidnapped," Lyranel said darkly. "He was going to pretend to save me, so I would see him as a… a hero. But I escaped."

"That's where you fouled up his plans," said Cate. "He didn't expect you to take matters into your own hands. I think you took him by surprise. He didn't believe you'd knocked out a bear, remember? And he didn't expect Elsie to help, either."

"He wasn't asleep," said Lyranel. "He followed us."

"The toad," said Elsie, standing in Lyranel's open door. "Well, never mind him. Look who I brought!"



Four puppies squirmed in her arms, Dulce's children. Dulce herself trotted beside Elsie, with frequent looks upward at her new mistress. They had already named the four pups: Teeku, Lion, Ysabeau—and Adam. He was the smallest, but the most persistent, and Lyranel's favorite. Elsie handed Adam to Lyranel, who settled him in her lap and gave him a piece of leather lacing to chew on.

"Well, Elsie, are you ready to go to Gavanton?" asked Cate.

"Already packed," the girl replied. She put the other puppies down on the floor, plopped down beside them, and laid her hand on Dulce's head. Dulce licked her fingers. "Can I take her with me? Or one of the puppies?"

"You may have pets at the Hall," Cate reassured her. "As long as you look after them."

"Do your parents know where you're going?" asked Lyranel.

"Aye," said Elsie. "Your father sent that Toby fellow to tell 'em." She grinned suddenly. "Didn't know what to make of him, they didn't. My Ma nearly skewered him, your Da said."



Lyranel snickered.

"Did they accept the land settlement from the Duke?" asked Cate.

"They're still negotiatin'," said Elsie.

"I thought you weren't going to Gavanton," Lyranel teased.

"Eh," said Elsie, shrugging. "I reckon I could use some training. I, uh, don't want to end up like… you know."

Lyranel nodded. She meant Lord Evander. "I don't think you would. It wasn't his lack of training that made him what he was. It was his attitude."

"Entirely true," Cate added. "He had a twisted mind. I think maybe because of what happened at his birth."

Both girls looked alert. "What?" asked Lyranel.

"The old Duke Candelo was a proud and arrogant man," said Cate. "He only let us Singers Sing for the current Duke when he was born because it was conventional. There were several children after that, but they all died or were stillborn. He blamed the Singers. When Evander came along so many years later, the old Duke refused to have him Sung into the world."



"So he never truly became part of the world's harmony?" asked Lyranel.

"Perhaps," said Cate. "We Sing for many babies, but there are also some born without it. They don't necessarily turn out the way he did."

"Not the training, eh?" said Elsie, with a sly glance at Lyranel.

"You still need to go!" said Lyranel, alarmed.

Elsie waved a hand at her. "I know. Don't get your knickers in a twist."

"They'll be glad to see you there, Elsie," said Cate. She turned to Lyranel. "You really stirred them up at the Singers' Hall, you know. Director Tyra says they'll be studying the implications of you and others actually hearing the voice of the *land* for years."

"Why couldn't I hear Candelo before I was kidnapped?" asked Lyranel.



"Perhaps because you were so busy with your studies," said Cate. "You weren't in the mood to listen."

"To anyone," Lyranel agreed, smiling at her teacher.

There was a knock on the door, and Nan bustled in, basket in hand. "All right if I join you ladies?" she asked.

"Of course," said Lyranel. She had been relieved to find Nan Sung back to health when she had returned to Castle Trioste. The Gavanton Singers had done a good job, Nan had said. In fact, she looked healthier than she ever had.

"What's that?" asked Elsie, when Nan had sat down in Lyranel's one comfortable chair and pulled a piece of white fabric out of her basket.

"A shirt," said Nan. "For Fergus." She held it up. There was mostly-finished embroidery on the cuffs and collar, of finely-detailed red roses.

"Fergus? The guard?" asked Lyranel. "It's beautiful. Why are you making a shirt for him?"

"Oh, well," said Nan, her cheeks turning a deep pink. "He has nothing fancy, you know."



Nan, blushing? Lyranel had never seen her nurse like this. Could it be love? Nan wasn't that old, really. In fact, Lyranel realized, Nan would actually be a few years younger than Lyranel's mother, had she still been alive. Nan picked up her needle and started to embroider tiny green vines between the flowers.

There was another knock on Lyranel's door. "Yes?" she called out. "Come to join the party?"

Elsie giggled, but sobered when she saw who it was. Duke Trioste stepped into the room.

"Father?" asked Lyranel, smiling. Elsie, Nan and Cate started to rise, and Lyranel reached for her crutches, but the Duke held up a hand, palm outward. They all settled back where they were.

"May I come in?" he asked.

"Certainly," said Lyranel.

He strode to her window, hands clasped behind his back. He was dressed in his ducal finery, from coronet to polished leather boots. The only difference was that today his outfit was a dark blue, instead of black. He took the chair from Lyranel's dressing table and put it near the window bench, then sat. He smiled briefly, watching Adam play with the leather lacing. When he reached out, the puppy sniffed his hand, then went back to his toy.

"Adam," said Lyranel's father. "A fine name for a fine dog. A fine man, too. I thought he had died when your mother did."

Lyranel shook her head. "No, he lived. And hunted Lord Evander, though he didn't know who it was at the time."

"Neither did I." Her father stroked the puppy's silky ears. "I knew someone had to have killed Miriana, you see. She wouldn't have let an accident like that happen to her."

"But, Rat, I mean Adam, said that she was tired after a long Singing," said Lyranel.

"She was a strong Singer, Lyranel, with close ties to the land. Even tired, she would have sensed if a rockslide was going to happen. Unless it had been caused by someone — or something — unnatural. At the time, I suspected it was a Singer. A jealous one, perhaps. I didn't know who, though." He glanced at Cate, and his smile tilted. "I even thought it might be you, Lady Caterina."



"I know," said Cate, quite calmly. "Tyra, the director of the Singers' Hall, let me see the previous director's records. Finally."

"So you understand why I banned Singers and endangered the Compact, then?" asked Lyranel's father. "I reported my suspicions to old Guerdelon, but he wouldn't do anything."

Cate nodded. "Guerdelon suspected a rogue Singer as well, but he couldn't let that knowledge become public. It would have caused panic in the streets, if anyone knew that it was possible for Singers to be willfully destructive."

"I thought the killer might come after you next," he said to Lyranel. "So to keep my little daughter safe, I banned *all* Singers from my lands.

"They didn't all go, though," said Lyranel.

"Yes, and I'm grateful for it, though I was angry when I found out that Guerdelon had defied me," said her father.

"Guerdelon didn't want me to come back," said Cate. "He wouldn't tell me why he didn't protest your decision, though. I yelled at him and tore out of there. I was surprised that he didn't protest when he found out where I had gone and what I was doing. I guess he couldn't really argue with my decision. Besides, I blamed myself."



"It wasn't your fault," Lyranel protested.

"I felt it was. I thought, if I had taught her better, she wouldn't have died."

Duke Trioste shook his head. "The blame lies squarely on Evander's shoulders."

He put his hands on his thighs and pushed himself up. "Well. It is near time for our Midsummer's feast to begin.

May I have the pleasure of your company this evening, my daughter?"

"Father..." Lyranel began. "You know that I have to go to Gavanton. I do need the training, still. And Singing... it's what I have to do. What I was meant to do."

"I know, dear one. This time, I have no worries. You will be a fine and powerful Singer, just like your mother."

"I'll have to give up my duties as Lady of the Castle," said Lyranel.

"Alistair will just have to live with that," said her father. He bent low and kissed her on the cheek.



The Great Hall was filled to capacity when they arrived an hour later. Lyranel and her father led the way, followed by Cate, Nan and Elsie.

"Relax," Lyranel whispered, when she noticed Elsie was twisting her fingers around each other.

Malcolm announced them all. Elsie blushed crimson when her name was read out as 'Elsie of Firwood'. The Duke led them all to the High Table, where he seated all but Nan as his honored guests. Nan had been asked to join them, but she had told the Duke that she would rather sit at a lower table, if he didn't mind. Lyranel smirked when she saw Nan sit next to Fergus, proudly wearing his new shirt.

Lord Mikal and his father, Duke Vierre, were also at the High Table. Mikal's father looked a lot like him, although stockier. Mikal's mother sat beside her husband, and a tall girl sat between them, her eyes bright as she looked around the room. She smiled when her gaze found Lyranel. Mikal looked decidedly glum. With his sister Sapphira back in full health, he was no longer first in line to become Duke. Lyranel had spoken with Sapphira earlier. She told Lyranel she knew it was Candelo, the land, calling her, but her father had shut her away before she could respond.



Their father was talking with Sir Thomas and Lady Joella. The two of them were going to take Nan with them when they left, as nurse to their child. Children, Lyranel silently amended. Lady Joella was expecting again. Glancing at Nan and her friend, she wondered if Fergus was going too.

Duke Candelo was not there, however. He had declined the invitation, saying that he was busy repairing the damage to his land, and helping his people to regain what they had lost. And perhaps he was mourning his younger brother.

When everyone was settled, Cook popped his head out of the kitchen door and peered at the Duke, who nodded. Lyranel knew he had planned to send out several of his creations this evening. She hid a smile. Paul had confided that there weren't any bears in his plans.

Cook disappeared and Paul emerged, carrying the front end of a laden trestle. Another kitchen boy carried the back end. Murmurs arose as the subtlety went past the tables, on its way to the High Table. The subject was a man, dressed in the uniform of the Duke's guards, his hand resting on the head of a droopy-eared dog. It was made entirely of marchpane—almond paste—painted with bright colors.



Lyranel's father rose, gesturing that everyone else should stay seated.

"Many of you will not remember my faithful guard, Adam," he said. "He was assigned to guard my wife, and he was there when she died, so long ago." Several gasps arose from the audience at this. "He blamed himself for her death, so my daughter told me. More recently, he redeemed himself when he made sure that her murderer was defeated. So we honor his memory. He is the subject of this masterpiece. He will be remembered with love and gratitude." The Duke lifted his goblet towards the sculpture and drank.

"Hear, hear," said Sir Thomas, as he followed suit, along with everyone else.

"There was much bravery that day," said Duke Trioste. "From such as my own daughter, Lyranel the Singer."

There was a roar of approval and Lyranel felt the heat rise in her cheeks.



"And there were others who were brave, too. Elsie, who was first her captor, and then her friend," the Duke continued. Elsie gulped and Lyranel squeezed her hand. "And the Singer Annice, who stayed in Candelo, to help its Duke in his work. But there was also one other. I would like to reward him for his great bravery."

The Duke leaned forward across the table and beckoned to Cook, then whispered something in his ear. Cook's eyes opened wide. He looked horrified, then resigned. With a heavy sigh, he walked to the front of the subtlety trestle and nudged Paul out of the way. He pointed with his chin at the Duke. Perplexed, Paul let go and faced Lyranel's father.

"Paul," said the Duke, "you came to us a long time ago, and proved a willing, helpful apprentice to our good Cook. It is to my great regret that I now must dismiss you from my service."

"What?" said Paul, his voice cracking. "I-I mean, p-pardon, Your Grace? Have-have I done something wrong?"

Duke Trieste's eyes twinkled. "No, boy. Something very right. You insisted on following my daughter after her abduction. You also followed her to my knight's manor, tenacious in your quest to find her. Then you accompanied her on her great work. You even tried to defeat Lord Evander when he would have overwhelmed Lyranel, even though you knew what his Singing could do. That was perhaps foolish, but no one can deny your bravery. Such bravery should not go unrewarded."



Paul glanced at Lyranel. She gave him a tiny shake of her head and widened her eyes. She had no idea what her father planned for her friend.

"Um, thank you, Your Grace," said Paul. "I… I need nothing. Really."

"Don't tell me what you need, boy," said Duke Trioste. He twitched one of his eyebrows. "I'll do what I wish. I've proven that before." He eyed Paul, whose Adam's apple bobbed up and down. "Well. You're over-old to become one of my pages. Sir Thomas? Are you in the market for a new squire?"

Lyranel gasped. A squire? That was the road to knighthood! Paul blinked and the color drained from his face. He looked about ready to drop.



"Mm," Sir Thomas mused. "Well, he's a bit scrawny. And I don't know if he'd want to trade in that useful long knife of his for a sword."

Paul held his breath, watching Sir Thomas.

"Still, I think I could train him. He's a fine young man." Sir Thomas turned to Lyranel's father. "I'd be honored to have him as my squire, Your Grace. Will you, Paul?"

"I-I. . ." Paul began, then a big grin spread across his face. "Yes!"

Cheers and applause rang throughout the Great Hall.

"Now, go get your things and put them in the outer room of our guest quarters. You can sleep there. I'll need you first thing in the morning, and I don't want to have to go looking for you."

"You will?" asked Paul.

"Oh, yes," Sir Thomas said with a wicked grin. "You'll be working harder now than you ever have."

"It can't be worse than the kitchen," said Paul.



Laughter rose from the audience. Cook glowered, then smiled at Paul.

"Go," he said. "I'll find another apprentice. I hope you know, Sir Knight, that you will be getting a good cook in this squire. You will eat well."

Sir Thomas smirked. "Why do you think I was so eager to take him on?"

Cook snorted. Paul grinned at Lyranel and she smiled back. His gaze slid to Lord Mikal, whose jaw hung open. Paul's smile twisted into a smirk. Lord Mikal shut his mouth with a snap, and inclined his head.

"Well, go on, boy," said Sir Thomas.

Paul bowed towards the High Table, then pelted out of the Hall. Even with the heavy doors closed, Lyranel heard a loud "whoop!" from beyond them.

She glanced at Nan, whose hand had been captured by Fergus, and then at Cate, who nodded. Then she looked at her father.

"Go ahead," he said softly.

Lyranel rose, braced herself on her crutches and Sang. It was a Song of happiness, for herself and her friends. It burst out of her and washed over everyone in the Great Hall, a Song of joy, of welcome, of life itself. It was Lyranel's Song.



*The End.*

## About the Author

*Leslie M. Carmichael has been inside the Great Pyramid at Giza, watched the moon cover the sun during a total solar eclipse, and been an honored guest at a Canadian-Scottish-Chinese wedding. She has swum in the Red Sea and the Mediterranean, picked amethysts out of the ground near Thunder Bay, watched a space shuttle land, and cooked a Medieval dinner for 200 people. At various times, she has worn a corset, a suit of armor and a Klingon outfit.*

*Leslie likes to travel, and work on miniature dolls and dollhouses when she's not writing. She has an impressive collection of costumes, which were made for plays, entering science fiction and fantasy costume contests, and pretending to live in the Middle Ages as a member of the Society for Creative Anachronism. She has even made costumes for some of the plays she has written.*

*She does cross-stitch (there's a picture of St. George and the Dragon above her computer that took five years to do), embroiders, and can crochet three-dimensional objects without a pattern, but finds knitting way too complicated. She sings soprano in a choir and loves just about any type of music, especially gospel.*

*Her Tai Chi instructor calls her writing "very yin-yang" (balanced), since it travels across the continuum from comic interactive mysteries to children's books.*

*This is her first book for children.*

# About Blooming Tree Press

◇◇◇◇◇◇◇◇◇◇◇◇◇◇◇◇◇◇◇◇◇◇◇◇◇◇◇◇◇◇◇◇◇◇◇◇◇◇◇◇◇◇◇◇◇◇◇◇

*Creating Hope*
*Encouraging Dreams*

Blooming Tree Press is located in the beautiful city of Austin, Texas and is dedicated to publishing quality books for young readers and adults.

The company is named after an inspiring woman, Mildred Bloom, who in her ninth decade continues to encourage and create hope in all who are fortunate enough to know her.

Blooming Tree Press will continue to offer adventure, mysterious excitement, hope and wholesome reading for the young and the young at heart.